The DEVIL'S EYES

In the President's Service: EPISODE 5

Ace Collins

Elk Lake Publishing

THE DEVIL'S EYES *In the President's Service: Episode Five*

Copyright © 2013 by Ace Collins

Requests for information should be addressed to:
Elk Lake Publishing, Atlanta, GA 30024
Create Space ISBN-13 NUMBER: 978-1-942513-10-0

All rights reserved. No part of this publication, either text or image may be used for any purpose other than personal use. Therefore, reproduction, modification, storage in a retrieval system or retransmission, in any form or by any means, electronic, mechanical or otherwise, for reasons other than personal use, except for brief quotations for reviews or articles and promotions, is strictly prohibited without prior written permission by the publisher.

Cover and graphics design: Stephanie Chontos
Editing: Kathi Macias
Cover Model: Alison Johnson
Photography: Ace Collins
EBook Conversions: Elk Lake Publishing
Published in association with Joyce Hart of Hartline Literary Agency

To Allison

CHAPTER I

Thursday, April 9, 1942
Noon
Outside Springfield, Illinois

There is a very thin line between nightmare and dream, fantasy and reality, or even sanity and insanity. In the more than two hours spent in his hidden treasure room, Fredrick Bauer wavered between those opposing elements of life's extremes. As he relished in the aura of all he'd gained, he also fully understood all he'd lost. And it was the losing that nibbled at his mind, consuming it piece by piece, pushing the reality of this world out and allowing an invasion of fantasy he could not control. And the trigger was looking into a face that was now little more than a grotesque and macabre rendering of what an unforgettable woman had once been.

While there was still no sparkle in her eyes or breath on her lips, this time she was no longer simply helplessly sitting and vacantly looking at him. As he sat in a chair, just ten feet from her body, with no warning a nightmare exploded like a toxic cloud enveloping his psyche until he could no longer distinguish between light and dark. While she had not reclaimed her beauty, she had found her voice. And though he knew it was impossible, he could hear her urging him to right the wrong done to her so many years before. That demand for vengeance started as a whisper but slowly grew louder until he had to cover his head with his hands before it shattered his eardrums. That's when he realized he'd crossed over to a world where sanity no longer dictated his moves. Jerking his head to the right, Bauer looked at his image in an antique mirror once looted from a castle just outside of Paris; the face reflected in the ancient glass defined madness. The eyes were aflame, the mouth twisted, the jaw gaping open, and the skin gray and drawn. Could this be him in the flesh, or was he finally getting a glimpse of his soul? Horrified at the image, he collapsed to his knees, pitched forward onto his face, and fell into a deep and troubled sleep. It was there, caught in a world that seemed so foreign and yet so real, that he and the woman once more lived and loved. Their spirits danced and their voices sang, as clouds of mist swirled all around them and, as if teasing him, she hovered just out of his reach.

Finally, after what seemed an eternity of pleading, she approached and he felt her hands on his neck. Just as her lips drew near his, he was jolted from his slumber by a demon he could not see but instead felt. Eyes suddenly wide open, Bauer found himself on his knees, just inches from her monstrous, mummified face. Repulsed, he twisted to quickly scan the room to see who had pushed him forward. Yet beyond himself and

THE DEVIL'S EYES *In the President's Service Series: Episode 5*

the woman who had not spoken in more than a decade, no one was there. He was alone. But rather than bring him comfort, the solitude proved the most unsettling sensation he'd ever experienced. What was happening to him? He had to regain control. He couldn't slip into the darkness that had claimed his father.

Though everything in his being begged him not to, his dark, brooding eyes, illuminated only by the floor lamp, fell back upon the woman. She appeared to be smiling, but she couldn't be. The look on her face had to be the same as when he had pulled her from her grave. Didn't it? Wasn't her death mask eternal? It had to be!

As he continued to stare into her lifeless eyes, he thought he heard her once more speaking to him. As her voice registered in the blackest corners of his mind, panic set in. Pushing himself from the floor, he lurched backwards, falling into a Da Vinci canvas. Catching himself on a support beam, he whirled and, wild-eyed and disheveled, sprinted to the steps. He took the stairs three at a time; only when he was back in his office and the bookcase was once again closed and locked did he take a breath. Raking his hair off his brow with his right hand, he crumpled breathlessly into his desk chair. For the moment, his heart quit racing and his emotions were once again in check. Then again he felt her cold, unrelenting stare.

Looking to the photograph, he focused on her image. Over and over again he whispered, "You're dead, you're dead, you're dead," and yet each of his begging pleas was immediately answered with, "I'm not; you just have to look for me. I'm waiting for you. You'll find me." Even though he knew it was impossible, he heard her scream those words over and over again, each verbal volley louder than the previous one. He continued to hear them even as he got up, raced out of the room, down the hall, and through the back door. After darting across the yard and into the barn, he worked the controls that opened the entry to his laboratory. When the steps were revealed, he rushed down them and over to a tall, stern woman standing by her desk. Her eyes disclosed she was completely perplexed by the man's seemingly panicked state.

"Emma, how are things?" he asked almost breathlessly.

"Fister is packed and ready," she assured him. "Nothing else is unusual."

"Good," he replied, his tone a bit stronger, though his knees were still as wobbly as Jell-O.

Sinking into a chair beside the woman's desk, Bauer took a deep breath and listened to the almost complete silence surrounding him. The haunting and demanding voice was gone; it had not followed him to the barn. The nightmare was over.

"Do you need anything from me?" Emma asked.

His heart rate slowing, his blood pressure falling to normal, Bauer glanced over to his assistant. She was dressed as usual: white blouse, dark skirt, and hose and flats. Her jet-black hair was pulled into a bun behind her head, and her face showed no signs of any makeup. Nevertheless, at this moment, she was the most welcome sight in the whole world.

"I'm fine. I just came over to check on things."

"So, will you be conducting any lab work today?"

THE DEVIL'S EYES *In the President's Service Series: Episode 5*

"No," he quickly replied. "Emma, I think I need to take a break. Been working much too hard over the past few days. I believe I'll just do some reading today."

"I finished putting together the file on the late Helen Meeker. It's on my desk if you want to review it before I put it away."

"It this it?"

"Yes."

Bauer reached over and retrieved the folder. While it was true that life would be much easier without Meeker gumming up the works, in a perverse sort of way, he hated to see her die. She was the first person in more than a decade that truly offered him a challenge. He'd even yearned to meet the woman and share his admiration for her brains and instincts before he had her killed. Yet the unexpected plane crash robbed him of that opportunity. And that was a real shame.

Opening the file, he glanced through the newspaper story rehashing the fatal crash. He was about to move to the next reports gathered from his intelligence sources when his concentration was broken by a voice.

"What did you say, Emma?" he asked.

"Nothing."

A quick look around the large underground chamber assured him the two of them were alone. Yet he felt another's presence, and he was positive he'd heard a voice. He'd stake his life on it.

"You found me," someone whispered.

A quick glance toward Emma, whose nose was buried in a magazine, clearly showed she wasn't the source. And she obviously hadn't heard the voice either. Even as he watched his assistant wet her finger and turn a page, he heard it again. Once more it demanded he do something.

"Ricky, look at the photograph."

Only one woman had ever called him Ricky, and she was locked in the treasure room. There were no such things as ghosts, so it couldn't be her. But who else could be playing this ghoulish trick on him?

Again the voice insisted, "Ricky, look at the photograph."

His eyes fell once more to the file. Beside the story of the plane crash was a headshot of Helen Meeker. As he studied it, the voice returned.

"Look, Ricky, doesn't she look like me?"

He realized then why she'd urged him to view the newspaper story more closely. She was right! Meeker did look like his Gretchen. The resemblance was uncanny. They could have been the same person. But that was impossible! Only a fool like Hitler or maybe a person locked behind the walls of a sanitarium would believe something like that.

"Ricky, it's me," the voice whispered. "It's me! It's me! It's me!"

Then the nightmarish vision grew even more ominous and haunting. Had she come back to him just to be killed in a plane crash? Had fate again robbed him of the only woman he'd ever loved?

His heart pounding so hard he felt sure Emma would hear, Bauer yanked himself upright and, after clutching the file to his chest, raced up the steps. He was back in the house and behind his desk before he once again found the courage to more closely

THE DEVIL'S EYES *In the President's Service Series: Episode 5*

examine Meeker's photo. He then looked to the framed picture on his desk. The hairstyle and clothing were different, but the face was the same right down to those unusual upside down dimples.

"I've lost you again," he whispered, tears filling his eyes.

"No, you didn't," she answered, this time in a soothing tone. "Ricky, I'm alive. You just need to look for me."

Was this insane assurance true? Did Meeker really die in the crash? Was the woman he once wanted to kill now the very one he needed to bring real substance, joy, and happiness to his life?

Once more he compared the photographs. The resemblance was unnerving. But it was more than just appearance: they were also brave, intelligent, and driven. They were more than somewhat alike; they were *exactly* alike. Could Gretchen have come back as Meeker, and could Meeker still be alive? There was only one way to find out. While it would demand his taking a risk and getting his hands dirty, he was going to have to dig up a fresh grave. If it was empty, then the voice was right; maybe a very live woman could replace the decaying body in the treasure room. But that was madness…wasn't it?

CHAPTER 2

Friday April 10, 1942
10:17 AM
Airport, Austin, Texas

For two full days Clay Barnes and Reggie Fister traced down leads on privately owned Cessna planes in and around Austin, Texas, and drew nothing but blanks. They'd even flown up north to check out what was supposed to be a C-165 Airmaster housed in Waco. That plane turned out to be a yellow C-145. Returning to Austin, the pair landed the DC-2, and while the black plane was being refueled, made a long distance call to the White House. Alison provided the not unexpected news that Mills' research had also come up blank. There were no C-165s registered in Texas. The past two days had proven to be nothing more than a colossal bust.

An old man in gray coveralls was topping off the DC-2's fuel tank when Barnes and Fister returned to their ride. As the airport employee went about his job, the two men pawed at the tarmac with their shoes.

"Becca must have guessed wrong," Barnes groaned. "The plane must have turned either east or west after it dropped off the nun." The mere thought of the kidnapped woman's habit sent chills up his spine. "If the plane was hangered in this area, someone would have known about it. I mean, how many blue Airmasters are there?"

"None around here," the old man chimed in as he pulled the fuel hose from the tank. "Do you want your windshield washed? It looks a bit dirty."

"If you don't mind," Barnes replied.

"I can push the ladder over there; won't be any problem at all."

As the airport worker shoved the wheeled ladder to the plane's nose, Fister looked out into the bright sky, "So where do we go from here?"

"I'm guessing back to D.C.," Barnes said. "Let's just hope Becca and Helen came up with something on our mystery woman. Right now we're late in the seventh inning and haven't yet gotten a single runner on base."

"What's that?" Fister asked.

Barnes smiled. He'd forgotten the Scotsman had no clue as to the nuances of America's pastime. "Nothing, Reggie; just a bit of local slang." The agent turned his gaze back to the elderly maintenance man. "Thanks for the extra work. We appreciate it."

As the airport employee rubbed down the glass, he asked, "What kind of Cessna you looking for?"

THE DEVIL'S EYES *In the President's Service Series: Episode 5*

Barnes folded his arms. "A blue C-165 Airmaster." In the background a radio spit out the strains of Bob Wills and His Texas Playboys, performing *Worried Mind*.

Fister laughed. "Boy, that song's lyrics fit us to a tee."

"Hillbilly music is the music of pain and suffering," Barnes agreed.

"It's a great song," the old man said with a shrug. "Shame about the plane. I thought I might have been able to help."

"What do you mean?" Barnes asked.

"Well, I filled up a red C-165 about fifteen minutes ago. The pilot took off and headed west. He didn't tell me where he was going."

Fister looked over to Barnes. "He could have painted it."

"I'm betting he did," the pilot shot back. "You still got some money?"

"Yeah."

"Pay this guy, Reggie, and give him a tip. I'm going to get into our plane and go through the check list. We're flying west."

After Fister climbed on, Bauer took the black metal bird airborne and up to cruising height. Setting the course due west, he peeked at the Texas map he'd clipped to the instrument panel. "We're headed that way."

The Scotsman shook his head. "There's nothing out there. It's as if the world is void of life. It's like we're on a trip to nowhere."

"Yep, this is really where the west begins. It just gets dryer and more desolate the further we go."

"So, if there's nothing much this way, where do you think

he's headed?"

"Likely to a private strip somewhere," Barnes explained. "We've got a cloudless sky, there's very little wind, and I'm going to take this crate up as high as possible so we can get a wide view of the land. You take the right and I'll take the left; just keep looking for anything red on the ground or in the air. This isn't just our best lead; it's the only one. We have to follow it even if it means we're headed to the edge of the world."

Fister looked down at the wide-open, almost barren landscape and quipped, "Looks like that's just where we're headed."

CHAPTER 3

Friday April 10, 1942
11:24 AM
Brady, Texas

The DC-2 flew smoothly over the Texas plains, its motors purring like twin kittens. Everything was perfect except the search, and that seemed futile. In the hour they'd been airborne, the two had seen nothing resembling a private plane of any color, shape, or kind.

"What period are we in now?" the Scotsman asked. "And do we have a runner yet?"

"It's *inning*," the pilot noted, "not period. And the answer is the ninth, and we're down to our last out."

"I have to believe that's not good."

Barnes pointed down to the arid scene below. "That's a very lonely cow down there."

"Do you think he's lost?"

"I'm betting he knows where he's going," the pilot joked, "but the same can't be said for us. That animal will find a haystack long before we can find the needle."

"So, Clay, do we turn around?"

"Not giving up that easy," Barnes assured him as he steered the plane slightly toward the north. "According to the map, there's a small airport in Brady. We'll stop there and ask if anyone knows of a red or blue Airmaster."

Fister squinted at the flat land below. He watched two cars drive in a southwesterly direction on a straight patch of paved road before turning his attention to the area below the plane's nose. "That looks like a landing strip."

"Sure does. That must be the place. Let's set this baby down and stretch our legs. It would likely be too much to hope for that a café or diner would be within walking distance. As they say out in these parts . . . partner, I'm getting on the hungry side."

"Might want to put your stomach on hold," Fister suggested. "Look over by the metal building."

The pilot studied the scene that was coming nearer each second, his eyes first locked onto the metal building and then the plane beside it. It was a likely a C-165, and it was definitely worth a look.

"Reggie," Barnes said, "we might want to have our guns ready. Pardon me while I once more employ the local lingo: there could be a shoot-out coming."

After putting the DC-2 on the ground, Barnes taxied over to the shiny building sitting at the end of the tarmac. Shutting off the black bird's twin engines, he shoved his gun into his pocket,

THE DEVIL'S EYES *In the President's Service Series: Episode 5*

slipped out of his seat, tossed open the door, and led the way to the ground. As he marched toward the Cessna, Fister dropped in step beside him. Fifteen feet from the red aircraft's nose, Barnes stopped.

"Is it the right model?" Fister whispered.

"It's not only a C-165 Airmaster, but look at the rear wing on this side. A piece of red paint about the size of an orange has chipped off. What do you see?"

"Blue."

"Let's find that pilot."

Barnes turned his attention from the Cessna to the thirty-by-fifty building. Based on the rows of carefully stacked boxes visible through the two large open doors, it likely served as a warehouse for materials transported by air to Brady. Standing beside several cardboard boxes was a tall, lean man who looked about thirty, and a shorter, older fellow wearing brown cowboy boots. Of the pair, the older one was the only one sporting a smile.

"What can I do for you, boys?"

"Let me take this," Fister whispered. The Scotsman pushed his hands into the leather coat he'd appropriate from a pilot named Vandy and smiled. "Didn't think I'd see you again."

Recognition suddenly lit the tall man's face. As the stranger nervously shuffled on his feet, Barnes locked his fingers around his gun. His hand remained in his pocket, palm firmly placed on the revolver's handle, as he waited to gauge the stranger's response. There was none.

Unperturbed, Fister continued. "Has the cat got your tongue?

I figured you'd have some questions for me. After all, it hasn't been that long. And I watched you size up the package I had with me. So you have to be curious about what happened to it."

The man evidently had no interest in being hospitable. He remained as mute as a sleeping steer.

"I don't think he's excited to see you," Barnes noted loudly enough so that everyone heard.

"Well," Fister replied, "not sure why that'd be the case. He was paid well. Maybe he's just feeling a little guilty."

"Now, partners," the short man said with a smile, "I don't know what this is all about, but my name's Carson Wright. I manage this place, and Ralph here delivers stuff for me. The folks around here, like the doctor and vet, would have to wait for days for needed supplies if it wasn't for Ralph and his plane. Same goes for businessmen and ranchers. I can vouch for him being an all-right kind of guy."

"I'm familiar with Ralph's business practices," Fister chimed in. "Why don't you tell Mr. Wright here about the services you offered me?"

There was no response, at least not from the pilot.

"Who are you boys?" Wright asked, his tone now not nearly as friendly.

Barnes, his fingers still on his hidden pistol, smiled. "We just need to talk to Ralph about his plane. Got some business he might be able to do for us."

"Well," Wright chuckled, "I'm sure he'd love to visit with you about that. I'll just step over here to my desk and review the shipping records on what he just unloaded."

THE DEVIL'S EYES *In the President's Service Series: Episode 5*

As the small, round man shuffled off, his boots clicking on the concrete, Barnes and Fister slowly closed the distance between them and the pilot. It was the Scotsman who spoke first.

"Time to come clean."

"She told me to do what I did," Ralph replied, his voice low. "When she hired me, I had no idea what it was all about. She just called you a package. I didn't know there was going to be any gunplay." He paused and studied Barnes. "Wait a minute. Weren't you the guy who had the gun on the tarmac in Brownsville? What's going on here? When did you two team up?"

"Who was the woman?" Barnes demanded.

"I don't think he has to tell you anything else," Wright shouted, his voice now much larger than his frame.

Somehow the little man had snuck up behind them and had a double-barrel shotgun stuck in the middle of the secret service agent's back. Being outfoxed by a local was not one of Barnes' finer moments.

"You're making a mistake," a perturbed Barnes announced

"You're the one making a mistake," Wright assured him, his West Texas twang ringing across the plains like an off-key church bell. "Ralph's my friend, and you two are strangers. One of you even talks like a foreigner, and the other is obviously a Yankee. We don't cotton to either one of those types around here."

"This is bigger than you, Mr. Wright," Barnes suggested.

"Most things are. Now, Ralph, you want to get on your plane and fly on out of here. I'll cover them until you're gone."

There was no debate; the lean man raced to the Cessna,

scrambled in the door, and, as the three men on the tarmac watched, fired up his plane, taxied to the end of the runway, and took off. He'd been airborne headed west for five minutes when Wright dropped his gun to his side.

The second the metal barrels no longer pushed into his back, Barnes whirled around to face the small, stout Texan. "That was a stupid move. The man you just let go was involved in transporting a German spy."

"You government men?"

"Yes, we are. And if I didn't have to track down that fugitive, I'd show you a thing or two about justice. You'd be in a cell so far away from light you wouldn't have to worry about that bald head of yours getting sunburned until long after the war."

A disgusted Barnes spat on the ground before jogging over to the black plane with the Scotsman in close pursuit. By the time Fister closed the door, the motors were fired up and running. The DC-2 was halfway down the runway before the newest team member had secured his seatbelt.

"Can you catch him?" Fister asked, glancing out the window toward the west.

"Catching him is no problem. We'll be on his tail in less than ten minutes. But other than keeping an eye on the guy, we can't do anything from the air. We just have to wait for him to either find a place to land or run out of fuel. He had a full tank when he left Austin. He likely used a third of go-juice on the trip to Brady." Barnes glanced down to the map. "The direction he's now going means he might be headed for Fort Stockton. I don't think he has enough fuel to make it."

THE DEVIL'S EYES *In the President's Service Series: Episode 5*

"So he'll crash."

"There's plenty of flat places between here and there, more than you've ever seen in your whole life, so he can find a safe spot to put the plane down. But when he does, there's no place to hide. Just a matter of patience, Reggie; we'll get him no matter what he chooses to do."

CHAPTER 4

Friday April 10, 1942
2:04 PM
Crockett County, Texas

"Well, Reggie, he's going down," Barnes announced as he peered out the windshield. "The motor's still spinning and he's not dead in the air, so I'm guessing he's figured out he doesn't have enough fuel to make it much further. There's a dirt road in front of him; I figure he'll try to set down there."

"How about us? Can we land on the road as well?"

"No problem. We'll follow pretty close. It'll take us a bit longer to pull to a stop, so I'll set down a couple of hundred yards behind him. You need to have your gun and be ready to scramble out the door as soon I pull to a stop. I'll follow. In this wide-open territory, I don't think he could evade us for every long, but I'd rather not have to spend all afternoon chasing him across the desert. Or, to put it another way," he added with a wry smile, "I've never been bit by a rattlesnake and don't want to experience that now."

As the Scotsman readied his firearm, Barnes eased the black bird down toward the West Texas landscape. In front of him, the Cessna's pilot was attempting the same maneuver.

"He's coming in too steep and too hard," Barnes noted. He shook his head and shouted, "Pull up, you fool!"

Sadly the Airmaster's pilot couldn't hear the agent's warning, and apparently when he realized his mistake, it was a second too late. By the time he yanked his wheel back, the final course was set. As the small plane hit the hard, firmly packed dirt road, its nose pitched forward and the prop struck the ground. The propeller dug into the soil, and the tail kept moving skyward; the Cessna flipped over onto its top. A split-second later, the upended plane twisted sideways and skidded off the road into the barren field. Its long slide was just coming to an end when Barnes set the DC-2 safely on the ground. The black bird wasn't even completely stopped before Fister leaped out the door to the ground and, with gun drawn, raced the hundred yards to the crash site. He was trying to force the cabin door when Barnes jogged up and looked into the cockpit.

"There's no rush; he's dead. Neck's broken."

Fister stepped back, shook his head, and asked, "So all of this for nothing?"

The secret service agent shrugged and glanced around at the barren terrain before his eyes locked onto a large cactus. He pointed toward the huge spiny plant. "You ever seen one of those?"

"No," the Scotsman admitted.

"Then the trip wasn't for nothing. Besides, there might be

THE DEVIL'S EYES *In the President's Service Series: Episode 5*

something in the plane that'll help us track down that woman. Maybe together we can force the door open."

It took the pair four tries, but they finally manage to get inside the upside-down plane. It was a now fully focused Barnes, depending upon his Secret Service training, who yanked the billfold out of the dead pilot's pocket.

"His name is Ralph Mountry," Barnes read. "Address is listed as an RFD outside of Cedar Valley, Texas. He's twenty-eight, unmarried, no pictures of any sweethearts or kids, and no one listed that should be contacted in case of an emergency. Seems to be a loner."

"The cabin's clean," Fister announced. "Hardly anything other than some maps, a Snickers bar, and an empty Coke bottle. Oh, and this." He reached up to retrieve an item stuck between the top and bottom cushions of the front passenger seat.

"What is it?"

"A woman's compact," the Scotsman noted while turning it over in his right hand. "It's a fancy one too. And look, it's engraved with three initials…GAL."

Barnes smiled. "That part of the story fits. The kidnapped nun remembered the woman's name was Grace. Let me see it." The agent took the item from Fister and studied it for a few seconds, looking at both the front and back, before snapping it open. "There's a brand name here, and that might mean something. Perhaps Becca can trace down where the Elegant Beauty line of cosmetics is sold. Combine that with the name Grace and the other two initials on this case, and we might be able to trace down the owner. So it wasn't a wasted trip. You got to see a native desert plant, and we have our first real clue."

Fister nodded while moving his eyes back to the pilot, suspended by his seatbelt, still hanging upside down in his plane. "What do we do about him?"

"We do the morally wrong thing," Barnes advised.

"What's that mean?"

"We leave him just as he is and let someone else find him. That'll give us time to go back to Austin, track down where he lives, and carefully examine his personal belongings to see if we can get the rest of the name on the compact or the woman's phone number or anything else tying him to whoever it is your brother and his friends are working with. After that, we get back to D.C."

"Wish he didn't have to die," Fister observed. "There's been way too much death in my life lately."

"He didn't have to die," Barnes assured him. "He made the choice to run, and even if he didn't admit it, he also had to know the kind of people he was working with." Barnes stopped, spotting something lodged under the backseat. "What's this?" As the plane was upside down, the agent reached up and pulled a wrapped package into full view. He studied it for a second before retrieving a knife from his pocket and cutting into the brown paper. "Well, well! If this is what I think it is, Ralph was also smuggling heroin. Wonder if the cowpoke back in Brady who held a gun on us is involved." After shoving the small package into his jacket, he added, "This guy was no saint and was anything but innocent. I'm betting we find out Ralph Mountry isn't his real name, and whoever this guy really is has a record a mile long. Let's get out of here."

CHAPTER 5

Saturday, April 11, 1942
2:34 PM
Columbia, Missouri

Dr. Warren Williams' house was small, quaint, and dusty. Set on a quiet street about a mile from the University of Missouri campus, it was obvious from first glance the house was occupied by a single man who lived to work. Textbooks, maps, and historical journals were everywhere. Several stacks of books, piled nearly three feet high, covered the dining table, with more spread out on kitchen cabinets. The professor even had to remove a dozen periodicals from an Edwardian chair just for Alistar Fister to have a place to sit. After pushing a pile of newspapers to the floor, the bubbly homeowner took a spot on what had likely once been a church pew. It sat on one of the few opened spaces on the floor and by two windows on the room's outside wall.

"It's so good to have you in my home," Williams announced. He grinned and shrugged. "My mind isn't what it once was. Now remind me who you are again."

"Riley O'Mally. I'm with the Antiquities Research Foundation."

"Oh, yes," the professor replied as he shook his head. "A wonderful group. They have funded so many special projects over the years. My friend Edgar Kisser at the University of Nebraska earned one of your grants to study American Indians in his state. Incredible researcher! Perhaps you know him?"

"No, we haven't crossed paths. Before the war, I actually spent most of my time in Europe. So the States are new to me. Just kind of getting to where I can find my way around your large expanses."

"I understand," the man answered, his light blue eyes twinkling. "The history in Europe is so much older than ours. Though, in truth, the two regions intersect even more than most realize. I've discovered that in my work. So much of American history owes its very existence to explorers from Spain, France, and England."

The visitor smiled. "I understand you've done a great deal of studying Ponce de Leon and the Fountain of Youth."

Williams shook his head, pushed his back against the wooden pew, awkwardly crossed one leg over the other, and chuckled. "Well, you're half right. In truth, I really don't know much more about Ponce than most undergraduate history majors."

"But I've always thought the explorer and the fountain were connected."

"So do most historians, and they might be right; I could well be wrong. But I believe the explorer who might actually have discovered the location of the Fountain of Youth was not a Spaniard, but a Frenchman."

"Really?" While Fister was not the least bit interested in any of what the older man was saying, he was doing a good selling that he was. It was easy to see Williams was convinced the visitor was hanging on his every word.

"After Ponce's trips to America," the professor explained, "a French nobleman named Jean-Jacques Chavet made the trek to the south-central part of the New World. He likely landed in the area around what is now New Orleans and made his way up the Mississippi River. His trip was less about exploring or even getting rich than it was about escaping punishment for killing a nephew of King Louis XVI in a duel. They used swords. The fight was over a woman…Adriene Dumont."

Fister laughed. "So a woman was involved."

"Isn't that always the case? Anyway, legend has it that Dumont disguised herself as a boy, snuck onto the ship, and even became a part of the crew before developing a deadly illness when the men were exploring Central Arkansas. It was only while treating the woman disguised as a man that Chavet discovered her true identity. I'm sure it came as quite a shock. Sadly, according to the story, there was nothing that could be done for her. Supposedly, when she died Chavet buried his beloved Adriene on a mountain overlooking the Arkansas River."

Fister smiled. "I'm guessing, both by your tone and raised eyebrows, you are not fully buying into the legend."

"It's a nice romantic tale," Williams admitted, "but I don't think a woman that was so special she drove men to fight to the death for her hand in marriage could remain disguised as a man for months while working alongside that very man who killed for her love. I mean, can you imagine an actress like Carole Landis getting away with that? The crew would have pegged her before she'd been on the ship for five minutes. Besides, there are records in France of an Adriene Dumont marrying an Englishman, moving to London, and having a dozen children."

"So, how does this story tie into the Fountain of Youth?"

"Good question. I wish you were in my class. So many of my students never make connections unless they're talking about getting dates with young coeds. Anyway, the only surviving records of Chavet's trip to the area were found about twenty years ago in a small French bookshop just outside of Paris."

Williams rose from his seat, crossed the room to a desk that was all but hidden by stacks of books, opened a drawer, and pulled out a folder. With no explanation, he walked back and set the file in Fister's lap.

"Don't touch anything yet," the host warned.

As his confused guest looked on, the professor opened a file cabinet and pulled out two clean white gloves. Only after handing them to Fister did he explain. "The papers are delicate, so please put the gloves on as you look through them."

After once more taking his position on the pew, Williams continued. "Do you read French?"

"A bit," Fister admitted while slipping on the gloves, opening the folder, and pretending to study the journal. His host gave the

THE DEVIL'S EYES *In the President's Service Series: Episode 5*

guest a few moments to examine the pages before continuing.

"Mr. O'Riley, most of what you will read describes animal life, encounters with different Indian tribes, and the difficulties of exploring the region. But about halfway through the trek, Chavet speaks of something very remarkable. A member of the Caddo tribe, a beautiful woman named Kawutz, not only guided the expedition up the Ouachita and Arkansas Rivers, but she became very close to Chavet. In his notes, the very ones you now hold, the explorer professes his love for her. So that's the real romantic tale, not the one of the French woman who became the cabin boy."

"Fascinating," Fister agreed as he scanned the document.

"But it's not romance that brought you here or drives my research. Beyond the pages where he writes of his love for the Indian woman, the explorer reveals something else Kawutz shared with him. What she told the Frenchman must have stunned him like nothing he'd ever heard in his life."

No longer did Fister have to fake his interest; Williams now had his full attention.

"Mr. O'Riley," Williams continued, his voice now little more than a whisper, "this Caddo woman told Chavet of her relationship with another explorer of the New World. His name was the same as you brought up earlier — Hernando de Soto. She claimed to be with him when he died."

Fister shrugged. "I'll admit this Indian woman meeting two different explorers might be unusual, but I'm sure it wasn't unheard of. I mean, there were lots of explorers running around the New World."

"I'll explain what you're missing in a moment. I think what has you confused is your lack of background in American history. But first, let me give you a couple of other facts. History books record that Kawutz would also meet an American president — Andrew Jackson."

"When was Jackson born?" the visitor asked, still confounded on the reasons for his host believing this information was so out of the ordinary.

"1767."

"And when was Chavet's trip to America?"

"In the early 1700s, likely about 1705 or 1706."

Fister nodded. "So Jackson must have met her when she was a very old woman and he was a young man."

Williams raised his brushy eyebrows. "Actually, Kawutz met Jackson at the White House in 1836."

Fister shook his head, now thoroughly confused. "But that would have meant she was at least one hundred and fifty years old." He chuckled. "So, professor, you're pulling my leg and I fell right into your trap for a moment. How long does it take your students to catch on when you try this in your lectures?"

"No," the professor corrected him, his tone anything but humorous, "I didn't ever share this with any of my classes or even our university's professor. And I'm not pulling your leg. And you are nowhere close to the woman's correct age either."

"What? This is so far beyond belief that it doesn't even register as a bad joke."

"Then let me really pull your chain. Kawutz met Jackson in 1836, Chavet in 1705, and de Soto in 1541." As a shocked

THE DEVIL'S EYES *In the President's Service Series: Episode 5*

Fister, his mouth agape, looked back at Williams, the older man continued. "Mr. O' Riley, look at the copy of the photo you'll find behind the last page of Chavet's journal."

Fister quickly flipped the pages and stared at the black-and-white image. It was a professional studio portrait of a beautiful, raven-haired young woman dressed in what was obviously American Indian garb.

"She's stunning."

"Yes, she is," Williams agreed. "Now look at the name on the back."

"Kawutz," the guest whispered. "That's impossible."

"I would wholeheartedly agree with you," the professor replied before pausing to lick his lips. His eyes looked past Fister and into space as he added, "It's completely impossible unless it was this woman who drank from the Fountain of Youth."

Fister attempted to assimilate the information he'd been given. It simply couldn't be true. This was nothing more than a legend. The photograph must be that of a young Caddo woman whose name matched the others in the story. Maybe Kawutz was as common in the Caddo world as Mary or Martha was in America. Besides, a man with the academic background of Williams wouldn't be party to believing something like a woman living for centuries. So what was this all about? What was the real story?

"Professor," Fister asked, "what happened to the Kawutz in this picture?"

"She was struck by a car while visiting New York City in 1916. She died in a Manhattan hospital and was brought back to Arkansas to be buried, but no one knows where. It is the location of the grave that I believe I'm close to discovering. And I also believe, from what I've been told by a woman whose grandmother prepared Kawutz's body for burial, that a map, written on a leather hide, was buried with her. I think that map will lead me to the Fountain of Youth."

Fister's was a logical mind. He put no stock in fantasy or things he couldn't see. So there was no way this story could be true. But if it was and the fountain did exist, then perhaps his days weren't numbered in months or even a year. And if that was the case, then he might escape what the injections were doing to his body and have his revenge against Bauer. His sudden irrational hope drew his eyes to the photograph he held in his gloved hand.

"Professor, what does the name Kawutz mean?"

"There's an ongoing debate on that, but I believe, based on my study of the tribe's history, it means 'One Who Walks Forever.' Now have I shown you enough and have you heard enough to allow me to apply for a grant from the Antiquities Research Foundation?"

Fister nodded. "How much do you need?"

The professor stood, took a deep breath, and shook his head. As he wrung his hands, he whispered, "I could likely get by on ten thousand dollars, but I couldn't guarantee the results. Still, I feel I'm so very close, that amount might do it."

Fister smiled. "How about ten times ten thousand? With that amount, how quickly could you find the grave?"

Williams' jaw dropped. "A hundred thousand?"

"Yes."

THE DEVIL'S EYES *In the President's Service Series: Episode 5*

The professor scratched his brow. "Would you mind if we had to skirt some legal issues and bribe some people to get what we need?"

"No. That would be fine."

"And what if, when we find the grave, the Caddo tribe won't allow us to exhume the body? Then we would literally have to steal it. And even as badly as I want that map, with my academic reputation on the line, I'm not sure I could do that. But I can't know if my theory is sound unless I get to see the body and take that map."

"Don't worry about that," Fister assured him. "I'll get the body for you. Your hands will never get dirty and your reputation will not be soiled. Now, do you want the grant?"

The answer came without hesitation. "Yes!"

Fister reached inside the pocket of the tweed jacket Emma had chosen for him and yanked out an envelope. "You'll need to fill out these forms. When you're finished, I'll take them with me. You'll have the funding by this time next week. We'll want you to move as soon as you have the money in hand. We want results, and we want them fast."

CHAPTER 6

Sunday, April 19, 1942
6:45 AM
Chicago, Illinois

Bauer smiled as James Killpatrick pulled himself out of his 1939 Dodge sedan and ambled toward their meeting spot. The short, stocky FBI agent looked none too happy, which was anything but surprising. Killpatrick was a night owl and hated early-morning meetings, and this was the very reason Bauer had chosen this time.

"Why does it always have to be at the stockyards?" the agent grumbled. "Why not a good restaurant somewhere on Lake Shore, or how about Washington? That's where I spend most of my time."

"Jimmy," Bauer replied, "the cows don't care what they see and never repeat what they've heard. But I've found waiters tend to not only hear what their customers say but remember everything. There are a lot of folks in jail because they shared too much at a restaurant table. They should have met right here and they'd still be free. And on Washington...I really don't care much for it. The capitol lacks the real substance, integrity, and grit found here in Chicago."

"Fine," the agent grumbled. "I guess your logic is sound. Anyway, I take it you've got something the FBI might want to know."

"Haven't steered you wrong yet. So I have to believe it's always worth coming to see me."

"I guess so, but I'd rather do this at a different time of the day. The air just feels so blasted thin this early in the morning. It's a wonder I can breathe."

Bauer smiled as he turned to study the seemingly endless number of cattle pens. He kept his guest waiting for a couple of minutes before inquiring, "What's your assessment of the raid by Doolittle on Tokyo?"

"If you ask me, and I guess you just did, it was pretty much a waste of planes and men. We essentially destroyed nothing of value. To me it was nothing more than a public-relations stunt."

The tall man nodded and continued to study the cattle. "I can understand a practical man like you feeling that way. But the nation is celebrating a strike against the enemy. I also have a feeling that millions of Japanese are nervously looking at the skies, wondering when the next wave of bombers will arrive. And don't forget, the enemy will now have to focus on protecting its mainland. I'm sure they never believed the U.S. could mount a bombing attack on them. So while this airstrike might not change the course of the war at this moment, it does

THE DEVIL'S EYES *In the President's Service Series: Episode 5*

dramatically change the mindset." He paused, rubbed his jaw with his left hand, and added, "You see, Jimmy, it's not what can happen that's important; it's what you *think* can happen that really matters."

"Did you get me up before sunrise to discuss war strategy, or to give me some new information?"

"Jimmy, you're always so impatient. You need to learn to relax. Why don't you take a deep breath right now?"

"Oh, cut the bunk," Killpatrick demanded. "I don't care if you've studied all eastern philosophy; I hate the smell of the livestock, don't like early mornings, I'm not very fond of you either, and I don't want to take a deep breath. Now tell me why I drove forty minutes into the rising sun."

Bauer smiled. "Fine, we'll do it your way. This is why you're here. There's something on a mountain in Nevada that Hitler wants."

The FBI agent glanced up into the larger man's eyes. "I hope you can be more specific than that."

"What does the date January 16, 1942, mean to you?"

Killpatrick scratched his head. "It's my mother's birthday. How did you know that?"

"I hope you at least sent her a card."

"I took her out to eat."

"Good for you, Jimmy. But what I'm talking about is the crash that killed Carole Lombard. There was something on that plane that hasn't been found, and the Germans badly want that lost item."

"The crash was a tragedy. Not only did Miss Lombard and

her mother die, but so did the crew and several of our servicemen. Still, I'm sure of this: there was nothing of strategic value on that flight. I've read the records. I know that for a fact."

"As far as the Americans know," Bauer admitted, "you're right. But let me do a bit of backtracking so you can fully understand why Hitler disagrees. In August 1939, Leo Szilard and Eugene Wigner wrote a letter that was delivered by Albert Einstein to FDR. This led to the creation of the Manhattan Project."

"How do you know about that?" the agent demanded. "Most folks at the Bureau aren't even in the loop."

"How I know isn't important," Bauer continued. "What I actually know is."

Killpatrick exhibited a sense of heightened urgency. "Keep going."

"There was man on that flight, a U.S. Army private. He was carrying all the research that exists on the development of the atomic bomb. It was on microfilm and hidden inside a cigarette case with the initials CK on the outside. The man's body was brought down the hill, but the case wasn't with the body. I think you know what that means."

"It's still up there, and now that the snows are melting, Hitler's going to get someone up there to find it."

"That's plausible," Bauer admitted, "or one of the rescue crewmembers took what they viewed as valuable items from the dead bodies, and it was one of them. How many people were on the team that went up to Double Up Peak on the Potosi Mountain to the crash scene and brought the bodies back?"

THE DEVIL'S EYES *In the President's Service Series: Episode 5*

"I don't know," Killpatrick admitted. "Maybe a dozen or two."

"Have any of them died since then?"

The man frowned. "What are you saying?"

"Jimmy, it's far easier to kill people and search their homes than it is to track something down on a mountaintop. I'm just pointing out that Hitler might have people working on identifying those who were a part of the mission to see if they have the cigarette case."

"How would the Nazis get the names?"

Bauer lifted his eyebrows in a mocking gesture. "Most of those who went up there were later interviewed by the press. It was big news. The names were easy to obtain."

Killpatrick's voice took on a near-panic tone. "What if they already have the microfilm?"

"They don't. They didn't realize their man was on that flight until today."

"How is that possible?"

"Because the case was given to a G.I. to give to a friend. He was an unwitting courier. The Germans just discovered the case was not in the list of things found. Up until two days ago, they figured the FBI had it in their possession and just didn't know what they had. So thanks to me, you have a chance to beat the Nazis to the punch. And that could be far bigger than Dolittle's raid."

"Anything more?"

"That's pretty much it. I don't even know the name of the serviceman who was given the case. I just know he was a private and not a spy."

"I've got to get moving," the agent announced as he pushed past Bauer and hurried toward his car.

"Just a second, Jimmy," Bauer barked. "This time I need something out of you."

The agent stopped, a shocked expression etched on his face as he looked back. "You've never asked me for anything. Not once in all the times we've been meeting."

"No," Bauer admitted, "I haven't. This time I am. But I'm not asking for trade secrets. Just tell me about the death of Helen Meeker."

"It was in the newspapers. All the details were there."

"Where is she buried?"

"As I remember, in the family plot in New York. I saw her sister, Alison, photographed by the grave. I think it might have been published in either *Time* or *Life*."

Bauer, his face stoic, continued. "Was it in Saratoga Springs? I think I read that was where she was born."

"That's where the family's roots were," the agent replied. "The plot is somewhere in one of the historic cemeteries there, but I don't know which one. Shouldn't be hard to find, though." The agent shook his head. "Why are you interested?"

"Just followed her career. I admired her spunk, brains, and tenacity. I was saddened by her tragic and untimely death."

"Anything else?"

"No, that's it. Good luck, Jimmy."

Bauer watched the agent hurry away, jump into the Dodge sedan, pull out of the parking lot, and back onto the street. He watched until the car was out of sight. Now alone, he turned back toward the cattle pens, reached into his suit coat pocket, and pulled out a gold case. After retrieving a cigarette and pushing it between his lips, he lit it and took a deep draw, then glanced down to what he was holding in his left hand. As he ran his thumb over the letters CK inscribed on the center of the front of the case, he chuckled.

CHAPTER 7

Monday, April 20, 1942
5:15 PM
Outside Drury, Maryland

Becca Bobbs yanked off her pumps and collapsed on the couch in the living room at the team's headquarters. The petite blonde was frustrated. She'd spent the last two days trying to trace down the buyer of the compact Clay Barnes and Reggie Fister discovered in the Texas plane crash. While her twenty or more hours of digging produced a great deal of information on the general area the case was likely purchased, it did nothing to bring them any closer to the mystery woman who owned it. As she fumed, she quickly discovered the room's silence only pushed her deeper into a pit of exasperation. It was time for a mood swing.

Pushing her hair away from her face, she got up, walked over, and switched on the radio. As she waltzed back to the couch, Bobbs grabbed the most recent issue of *Newsweek* and flipped through the pages. Sinking back into the couch's deep cushions, she was reading a movie review when news of the war, blaring from the Zenith's large speaker, diverted her attention.

The Nazis pounded Malta today as Hitler tossed everything he had at the island located about sixty miles south of Sicily. Making sure the Allies are not able to control the Mediterranean Sea seems to be the Germans' aim as they attacked the small hunk of land in the middle of the large expanse of water.

Meanwhile the nation and much of the free world is still basking in the glow created by Dolittle's raid on Japan. While little is known of the damage done by the bombers, the mere fact that American air forces have shaken the island nation and its leadership has buoyed spirits from coast to coast.

"Didn't know you were back from D.C.," Helen Meeker announced as she swept into the room and broke Bobbs' attention.

Unlike Bobbs, who wore a dark blue dress suit and seamed hose, the barefoot Meeker was dressed in slacks and a sweater, her hair pulled back in a ponytail and her face hinting at only a trace of make-up. It was a casual look few, including her blonde friend, ever saw.

"I've been here for about twenty minutes," Bobbs replied, tossing the magazine back on the coffee table. "It wouldn't have hurt if I'd come back soon enough to take a nap. Pretty much wasted my time the past two days."

"So you didn't find out anything?" Meeker was obviously disappointed.

"Oh, I wouldn't say that. I found out a lot of things, actually. Do you know you can only purchase this compact on the West

THE DEVIL'S EYES *In the President's Service Series: Episode 5*

Coast and there are hundreds of stores that sell it there?"

"Good to know the next time I'm in California," Meeker quipped. "That is, if there is a next time."

"And I found a great deal on some lipstick," the blonde announced. "I bought a new suit as well. But sadly, we have nothing more on Grace. And as the guys couldn't find a single thread of evidence at the dead pilot's house, we're stuck. We don't even have anyone we can quiz. Now that you've heard my bad news, how did things go on your end?"

Meeker switched off the radio before dropping onto a light blue art-deco, cloth-covered club chair and crossing her legs Indian style. Once comfortable, she frowned. "Same as you. I went through every phone listing I could find connecting the initial L to the name Grace. There are hundreds. But none of them led to a woman with alabaster skin. I did find one lady that kept me on the phone talking for twenty minutes about the fact you can't get good produce in the stores anymore and another that was sure I was part of a radio quiz show. And because I was stuck here, working the phone, I didn't even get the benefit of getting any fresh air or checking out the latest things in the boutiques...like someone I know did. What color is your new suit?"

"Robin-egg blue," Bobbs replied absently before reverting back to the subject at hand. "Helen, with no fingerprints on the case other than Reggie's and Clay's, we have nothing to go on." She paused before making a verbal jab. "It was a shame you weren't with me. You would have loved the suits and dresses I saw in Ramone's."

"It's not like I'll be going out much," Meeker replied. "I mean, technically, I'm dead. And unlike you, I have to act like it. Must be nice not to be recognized."

"Right now living is overrated. And this woman we're looking for, the alabaster-skinned goddess I was twenty feet away from in Brownsville, likely knows what was in that tube Alistar Fister was carrying. She might even know the man who's pulling the strings behind this whole mess."

"Maybe we're reading far too much into this," Meeker cut in. "Fister's a lady killer. Perhaps he just met her in Texas and hitched a ride with a woman he found attractive. Maybe he didn't know she or the pilot was smuggling heroin. If she was just a one-night stand, perhaps Alistar used her to orchestrate his escape, meaning she knows nothing more than we do. Think about it. The dope could have been smuggled across the border and warehoused in Brownsville, and the ride Alistar caught was already there for the purpose of taking the stuff north. The woman might well be from the west coast, and she got her compact there. Our logic in this matter might not be logical at all."

"And," Bobbs sighed, wrinkling her small, perky nose, "if we think about it that way, then we are really lost."

She watched Meeker rise from the chair and walk back across the room to the Zenith console radio and switch it on once more. The tubes were still warm enough that the sound came up almost immediately. As the strains of Glen Miller's *String of Pearls* played, she returned to her chair.

"Good dance song," Bobbs noted.

THE DEVIL'S EYES *In the President's Service Series: Episode 5*

"Well, we don't get to dance much anymore, do we?"

Bobbs nodded and let her mind drift. She wondered if Clay danced. If he did, what kind of music did he like? Did he still think about that night in Brownsville? Did her kiss linger on his lips like his did on hers? She brought her fingers to her mouth and frowned. Neither one of them had said a word about that incident since they'd returned. It was as if it had never happened. But it had happened, and she wanted it to happen again. Was that wrong? Was she reading far too much into something that was originally intended only as a cover for a stake-out?

"You read today's paper?" Meeker asked, interrupting Bobbs' thoughts.

"Just glanced at the headlines. They're still playing up the Dolittle raid."

"It's even bigger news than the U-boat we caught."

"As I recall, the FBI took credit for that."

"Another disadvantage of being dead." Meeker smiled. "Reading the paper is depressing now."

"You mean the war news?"

"Yes. But we're also no longer free to live normal lives. I read about places I want to go and things I want to see, sales at stores, movies that have just been released, and it makes me realize that being cut off from the real world and working in the dark means we sacrifice a lot. I never even got to see *Woman of the Year*. But I shouldn't complain; just think of what the men on the fronts are giving up. We have it easy."

Bobbs nodded. "Kathryn Hepburn and Spencer Tracy were in *Woman of the Year*; I saw it the week it came out. Good movie, but in truth I'm more into Gable than I am Tracy. Wonder what's playing tonight."

Pushing off the couch she walked over to a library table at the far side of the room and picked up *The Washington Post*. She flipped through the pages until she came to the entertainment section. Her eyes dropped down the pages, looking for theatrical ads, when a gossip column caught her eye. She skimmed the first paragraph covering the opening of a new restaurant before spotting a blurb about the British Ambassador taking visiting dignitaries to a local club. People were being killed all over the planet and the world still played. It seemed even blackouts couldn't kill the nightlife. Was that good or bad?

"Helen," Bobbs asked, "what do you know about The Grove?"

"The nightclub?"

"Yes," Bobbs said as she carried the paper back to the couch.

Meeker shrugged. "Been open for years. Owned by a man named Dick Diamond. Supposedly he has connections to organized crime, but that's never been proven. The place has good music and food. I've been there a couple of times on dates. I wouldn't mind going back again."

"The club's featured in Bill Chance's *On The Town* column. Some British diplomats held a party there last night."

"Yeah, I've heard the Brits love the place. I likely met some of them when I was at their embassy."

"But listen to this," Bobbs announced and began reading out loud. "Our visitors from England could not stop raving about The Grove's floorshow featuring the club's headliner Grace

THE DEVIL'S EYES *In the President's Service Series: Episode 5*

Lupino. Lupino, so well known for her love of red dresses and big hats, charmed the honored guests by leading the audience in a rendition of *God Save the Queen.* After dining with the delegation from across the pond, Lupino insisted the Brits call her by her pet name, Gal, which all club regulars know is what you get when you combine her initials."

Meeker, fire coming back to her eyes, sat up straight. "The nun said she sang."

"And I saw our mystery woman dressed in red and wearing a big hat. There's a photo of her with the British ambassador, and she has the fairest skin I've ever seen."

"Becca, we need to do some homework on this songbird they call Gal. Where's Spencer? To do this right, we need a man for the job."

"In his lab. He's still trying to figure out what's in Alistar's blood."

"Well, his day is over. He's about to go clubbing."

Becca raised her eyebrows hopefully. "Does he need a date?"

"Yes, he does, but you'll have to stay home this time."

CHAPTER 8

Monday, April 20, 1942
8:15 PM
Washington D.C.

    Dr. Cleveland Mills adjusted his green-striped tie and smoothed his black coat before raising his hand and knocking on the door. He listened to the music being played by a swing band, tapping along with the beat until a voice on the other side called out, "It's open." Turning the knob, the White House physician apprehensively strolled into the office of Dick Diamond.
    Diamond was tall, thin, and dapper, about fifty, and looked as though he'd just stepped off the set of a Hollywood movie. His thick, dark hair was parted on the right, and his green eyes shone like fiery marbles. The nightclub owner was smoking a cigarette, wearing a tuxedo, and sitting behind a massive desk that was completely void of clutter. Expect for an ashtray, lamp, and two phones, the massive piece of walnut topping the impressive antique was empty. He was either extremely efficient

or had very little on his agenda.

"What can I do for you?" the owner asked as he snuffed out his smoke. "I hope you don't have a complaint about the food. The chef escaped the Germans and is very sensitive about people who don't cater to his cooking. The last man who ventured into the kitchen offering suggestions was chased three blocks down the street. That wouldn't have been so bad, but Phillipe was carrying a butcher knife as he ran. And it was a very large and sharp knife."

"The food was excellent," the guest assured him. "I'm here on another matter. My name is Dr. Cleveland Mills. I am FDR's personal physician."

"So you're making club calls now?"

"You could say that."

"You've got my attention. Pull up a chair and take a seat. I doubt if you came here to check my pulse. I'm pretty sure of that as most everyone in government wishes my heart would stop beating. So what's on your mind?"

The doctor made his way to a large, plush chair situated in front of the desk and eased down. After smiling, he announced the reason for his visit.

"There's a young man with me, and to put it bluntly, he's dying. Now I haven't told him he may have only months to live because I simply can't bring myself to break the heart of someone who has so much to live for. After all, this gentleman has money, breeding, an Ivy League education, and a great deal of charm."

Diamond leaned forward. "I'm sorry to hear that, but what can I do? I run a club, not a hospital."

THE DEVIL'S EYES *In the President's Service Series: Episode 5*

"Mr. Diamond, the president was wondering if you could possible send your singer—I believe her name is Grace Lupino—over to his table at some time tonight to meet him. He thinks the world of her. Maybe they could chat a little."

"Yeah," the host said with a shrug. "I can make that happen. You say the kid's out there right now?"

"Your staff told me he's seated at table eight."

"When Gal finishes, I'll have her go over."

"Thank you so very much," Mills announced as he pushed out of the chair. "I won't take any more of your time." The doctor ambled over to the door, twisted the knob, pulled it open, then turned back. "Mr. Diamond, the president has been made aware of an investigation looking into your ties with Lucky Luciano."

"Lucky's in jail," Diamond snapped back, suddenly sounding more than a bit agitated. Frowning, he rose from his chair, stood behind the desk, and folded his arms over his chest as if daring his guest to challenge him.

"I'm aware of that. But for some reason, the district attorney seems to believe Luciano is funneling money through this club."

"He's not," Diamond growled. "Dick Diamond has never been seen with Lucky Luciano."

"I know that, but Richard Powelletti has. And I think you have a working knowledge of Mr. Powelletti."

"What's your game?" Diamond demanded.

"You changed your name from Powelletti to Diamond. And you did it to try to cover your association with Luciano and several other members of organized crime. There's no reason to deny it; the president knows."

"Okay." Diamond shrugged. "I'll admit I once dabbled in some things on the wrong side of the legal tracks, but no more. Those days are long behind me. Five years ago I got a new name and a new life. And it's all legal."

"Would you take a lie detector test on that?"

"Yes, I would. I've offered to do that a dozen times."

"Then you'd like to see the D.A. pull back?"

"He's got nothing to find here," Diamond snarled, "but he still makes my life miserable. So of course I'd want him to pull back. In fact, I'd like him to back off so far he'd wade into the Atlantic Ocean."

The doctor grinned. "Mr. Diamond, you see that Miss Lupino shows the young man out there a good time, and I think the president will be able to shift the district attorney's vision. If you understand what I mean."

"Are you saying he'll get off my back?"

"I'm promising he'll be out of your life."

"What's your boy's name?" Diamond asked, the words now spilling from his mouth like water splashing over a dam during a flood. "I'll make sure he has a great time. In fact, he'll have the best time of his life."

"You can call him Jim."

The doctor nodded, closed the door, and walked down the hall and into The Grove's main dining area. He looked across the dance floor, caught Spencer Ryan's attention, touched the index finger of his right hand to his brow, then turned left and exited. It was now all up to the younger physician to dial up the right prescription.

CHAPTER 9

Monday, April 20, 1942
11:00 PM
Washington D.C.

Though it was supposed to be work, the first two hours of his first solo mission were the most fun Dr. Spencer Ryan had experienced since his college days at the University of Chicago. Grace Lupino had pulled out all the stops. She'd not just charmed him, but her flirting, which included whispering funny jokes in his ear and letting her fingers dance over his white dress-shirt collar, made him feel like a king. And when she'd paused to sing *My Man*, he'd felt as if the words were meant for him alone. If this was the life of a man undercover, he wanted a lot more of it.

"Jim," she whispered after she came back to the table, "I hope you liked my number."

The way she breathed the line had him wishing his name really was Jim. In fact, as the smell of lilacs filled his senses, the doctor almost forgot his cover. If he'd had a diamond ring, he might have proposed on the spot.

"I loved the song, Grace," he said, his throat as tight as a violin string.

"Call me Gal," she cooed. "All those really close to me do." She leaned over until their arms touched. "And I really want you to be very close to me. I can assure you, there is nothing in the world I want more than that."

It was just a line, he reminded himself. He knew she didn't care anything for him, but the way she delivered that line made his heart skip a beat. As thoughts of romance flew into his head, they pushed everything else out. If temptation had a name, it had to be Grace. There suddenly was no war, no mission, and no team. There was only this woman and the mystery and wonder she brought to this moment.

"Okay, Gal," he whispered. "I can't think of anything I'd like better than to be close to you."

"Let's get out of here," she suggested. "It's too noisy, and I so want to know you better. I can only do that when I can listen carefully to each and every wonderful word you say. And with the orchestra playing so loud, we can't do that here. Are you ready to leave and go someplace with low light and no one else but the two of us?"

"Where do you want to go?"

"How about your place?"

Those words woke him up to who he really was and caused him to reclaim his cover. This was all a ruse; he had no place to go to, nowhere to take her. "I'm sorry," he stammered as he

THE DEVIL'S EYES *In the President's Service Series: Episode 5*

scrambled to create a good lie, "but we can't go to my place. You see, my sister's in town and she brought a couple of college sorority sisters with her, so it would be louder there than it is here."

Lupino ran her fingers up his neck and gently pushed them through his hair. She allowed them to linger on his scalp for a moment, licked her lips, and leaned so close he could feel her breath on his cheek.

"I've got a nice apartment," she cooed. "You could tell me all about your life. I want to hear every tiny detail. I just can't believe I'm with a great-looking guy who knows the president. This is like I was offered one wish and it came true."

"The wishing goes both ways," he assured her.

"You stay here, and I'll get my coat. The night's young, and I want to spend every moment of it with your eyes locked on me."

She seemed to float from her chair, all the while keeping her dark eyes honed in on the man, before turning and sashaying across the dance floor. All but hypnotized, the doctor's gaze followed the sensual movement of her form-fitting red dress until it disappeared through the backstage door. His eyes remained glued to that spot until a few moments later when she reappeared, a coat tossed over her shoulder, and waltzed back to the table and grabbed his hand. As she gracefully led Ryan across the crowded room, every eye in the place followed the woman's cat-like movements. Lupino had so much exotic oomph, a herd of elephants could have lumbered onto the stage and not a man in the place would have noticed.

A short cab ride led to the stylish and exclusive Red Rose

Apartments. The building was made of white stone and climbed seven stories into the Washington sky. After rushing through the entry, her arm in his, they grabbed an elevator ride that deposited the couple on the fourth floor. Lupino pulled her key from her small clutch, paused, and looked longingly into Ryan's eyes before pushing that brass key into the lock. After the door opened, she leaned into him, lifting up on her toes and offering her lips. She drew close, kissing him once, and then grabbed his gray tie and led him into a lavishly furnished flat covering more than two thousand square feet.

The unexpected kiss momentarily clouded Ryan's mind. Only when his date dropped his tie and turned on a lamp did he take his eyes off the woman to study his surroundings. Lupino's apartment was much like the singer. In all his years, he'd never seen anything like either of them. They both begged for attention while at the same time providing a sense of dangerous comfort. Decorated in various shades of red, white, and pink, filled with custom-made art-deco furniture, the flat looked like something a Hollywood set designer would dream up for a Technicolor film. The living room was so crammed with furniture it was hard to walk without bumping into something, reminding Ryan of a spider's web — unique, appealing, and deadly. Then a cold thought hit him: this wasn't as much a home as a feminine lair, and he'd fallen for the bait.

Lupino grabbed her guest's left arm and whisked him to a small but richly padded loveseat and then pushed him down. She leaned forward, allowing her hair to caress his face, and brought her lips to his once again. After a long kiss, she pulled

THE DEVIL'S EYES *In the President's Service Series: Episode 5*

back, smiled, and left the room. His mother had warned him about women like this. Those warnings, still fresh in his mind, demanded he run. Yet at this moment, his knees were way too weak to even lift him off the couch. Suddenly he knew how Samson felt when the strong man met Delilah.

Alone, Ryan shook the scent of intoxicating perfume from his senses and took stock of his surroundings. Rising unsteadily to his feet, he glanced into the kitchen. After studying it for a few moments, he stepped over to a door leading to a second bedroom. Flipping a switch, he noted nothing unusual other than this room had been decorated in shades of blue. In that sense, it didn't fit. Moving back to the loveseat, he eased down and pushed his back into the deep cushions. It was then he noted something so obvious as to be obscure. There were no paintings on the walls, tables, or bookshelves. The dozen or so frames in the room were filled with different images of Grace Lupino. The whole place suddenly took on the aura of a shrine.

"Hello again."

Glancing to the now open bedroom door, Ryan's eyes took in the woman behind the lush greeting. A bright red satin gown hugged her body like a road clung to a mountainside. It was just low enough to be enticing but not so low as to be scandalous. The slit in the bottom revealed a great deal of the woman's right leg and three-inch scarlet heels. As she glided past the couch, she turned slightly to show off the gown's low riding back. Lupino's alabaster skin glowed, and there was so much now on display it would likely take an hour just to map it. Ryan wondered if the person who designed this formfitting number had run out of material before they finished or if this was the way they'd intended to uncover the wearer. Whatever the reason, he wasn't complaining.

"I always get comfortable when I come home from work," she whispered as she eased down beside him. "I hope you don't mind."

"I don't mind at all," he said, his shaky voice showing a combination of both excitement and apprehension.

She laid her right hand on his neck, leaned closer, bringing her body into his, and chirped, "Tell me about yourself."

That was the cue he'd been waiting for. It was now time to invent the story of Jim Macon's life. Mixing elements from his own memories and coupling them to scenes from *The Great Gatsby,* Ryan wove a tale of adventure bought with the family's personal fortune. Between safaris in Africa, climbing mountains in Nepal, and skiing in the Alps, Jim's life was one that made Errol Flynn's look placid and boring. An hour later, when he finished telling a tale about escaping headhunters in the Amazon, she laid her head on his shoulder and nearly purred like a kitten. Her next words proved she'd taken the bait hook, line, and sinker.

"You're amazing. I have to get to know you better." Her lips found his cheek, lingering there long enough to leave impressions of her dark red lipstick. "I wish you could stay longer, but a girl needs her sleep. Maybe we can do this again tomorrow night. If you'd like that."

"I would," he assured her.

"Come to the club, and after my last song, just walk back to

THE DEVIL'S EYES *In the President's Service Series: Episode 5*

my dressing room."

She rose to her feet and floated toward the door. After opening it, she looked over her all-but-bare shoulder and smiled.

Taking the cue, Ryan pulled off the loveseat, moved quickly to her side, leaned over, sliding his right arm around her back, and drew her mouth to his lips. The kiss was long and passionate. When they broke, he pulled his arm back from her body. As he did, he thought he saw her eyelids flutter. Grinning, he turned and walked out the door and to the elevator. He would later swear his feet never touched the ground.

CHAPTER 10

Tuesday, April 21, 1942
11:12 PM
Washington D.C.

True to his word, Spencer Ryan was back at The Grove the next night. With Dick Diamond watching approvingly from the far side of the room, almost out of view by the right stage door, the doctor and Lupino talked and flirted between her numbers. But the club owner wasn't the only one watching; there was another set of eyes, this pair of dark blues unseen, following every move the singer made. After Lupino finished her final number, a slow version of "San Antonio Rose," she slipped off the stage, down the hall, and into her dressing room. She'd closed the door and was reaching to pull off her earrings before she realized she wasn't alone.

"Who are you?" the songstress demanded as she eyed an auburn-haired woman sitting at her dressing table.

"Does it matter?" Helen Meeker crossed her legs and let

the heel of her right pump dangle loosely. "I could be a million different people for all you know. I might even be a ghost. The key is that I'm here. At this point, that's all that matters."

"Who let you in?" a defensive Lupino demanded, her expression as cold as a Canadian lake in December.

"I let myself in. Locked doors don't keep me on the outside looking in; I open them almost as easy as I open people's minds and find out their intentions. Now sit down over there and we'll talk."

Shaking a finger at the intruder the singer warned, "I'm going to go get Dick and have you thrown out."

"Fine. Call Mr. Diamond. I can guarantee when he hears my story the only person who'll be getting kicked of this club is you. Right now I can do more to protect you than Mr. Diamond. Besides, the less he knows about your shady connections, the more likely you are to keep your well-paying job. Sit down, dearie."

Lupino was torn. She wanted to call the club's owner, but she was wavering. Who was this woman, and how dare she invade her private space?

"Okay, Grace, this is your dressing room and you're wondering why a woman like me is here. I get that. But let me assure you that it's in your best interest to let me say my piece." She paused and smiled. "If you don't, then the newspapers might be writing about a beautiful songbird whose voice suddenly stopped in mid-note. That's not a good way to end your life or career."

"Why come after me?" Lupino demanded. "Diamond might be mixed up with some shady types, but I'm on the level. I sing my songs, sign a few autographs, and stay as far away from trouble as possible."

"And," her guest added, "keep Washington clothing shops busy outfitting you in crimson threads." Meeker tilted her head. "You know what happened to the original woman in red?"

"No."

"She set Dillinger up. She thought she'd be a hero. Instead she was deported. Likely dodging Allied air attacks in Europe right now."

"I'm an American citizen. You can't deport me."

Meeker smiled. "But you can die, and that's far worse than being deported."

A knock on the door pulled her attention from her uninvited guest. Grabbing the knob, she swung it open, relieved to see her date for the evening standing in the entry.

"Jim," she cried, tossing herself into his waiting arms.

"As promised," the man announced with a grin. He looked past the singer to Meeker. "Who's your guest? Did I interrupt something?"

"She hasn't told me her name or her business," Lupino moaned as she pulled herself from the man's grip and turned once more to face the other woman. "And I'm growing very tired of her company."

"If she's bothering you," Ryan suggested, "I can usher her out."

"I wouldn't try that," Meeker cut in. A second later she produced her Colt, aiming it directly at Lupino. "Both of you, sit down. You," she said, pointing with her free hand to Ryan, "take a seat on the folding chair by the door. And Miss Lupino, you plop yourself down on the couch."

"I think we best comply," Ryan suggested as Lupino's hopeful gaze met his. "I'm not much into the type ventilation provided by flying lead."

"Okay, Grace," Meeker said. "I hope you don't mind me calling you that."

"Call me whatever you want as long as you leave me alone."

"I will in time," Meeker assured the woman as she reached her left hand into her coat pocket and pulled out a small, circular item. Waving it in the air she said, "I think this belongs to you."

"Did you steal that?" Ryan asked, his tone harsh and demanding. "Are you some kind of thief?"

"No," the visitor answered. "It was found in a Cessna airplane in Texas."

"I've never even been to Texas," Lupino declared, hoping her tone came across more confident than she felt.

"Then how did this get to the Lone Star State?" Meeker demanded.

"It's probably not mine," Lupino quickly explained. "Mine has my initials on it. I probably lost it somewhere in town. Like on a cab ride or during a walk in the park."

"This one has your initials engraved on the case," Meeker assured her. "I can read them if you wish. I doubt there are that many compacts that can only be purchased on the West Coast with your initials on them in Washington."

"Okay," the singer argued. "I told you I lost it. It's probably mine, but whoever found it must have taken it to Texas. As I said, I've never been there."

Meeker grinned. "Interesting that you've never been to a

place where this compact was found and where several people spotted a fair-skinned woman in red who loves big hats."

"I don't need the third-degree," Lupino blared defensively. "I'm respected in this town. People know me and trust me. I lost it, or it was stolen and then found in Texas. That's no big deal. But, I'll tell you what." Her tone grew softer. "I'll give you a reward for returning it to me."

"I don't want a reward," Meeker replied, her gun still aimed at Lupino's heart. "What I want is information."

Lupino was squirming now. "When did you find it?" she demanded.

"Let's just say you lost it about ten days ago, and it was found in an airplane in Texas."

"I tell you," Lupino argued, "I've never been there."

"That will come as a surprise to a nun who made a recent flight with you."

Grace felt the color drain from her face. For a full minute, she remained mute as she tried to come up with an explanation.

"I haven't been to Texas," the singer explained at last, "but I did ride in a Cessna about two weeks ago when I was in Mississippi. Was the plane blue?"

"It was."

"I must have dropped it then."

"And what about the nun?"

"I don't know anything about a nun. I'm not even Catholic."

The visitor shook her head, her dark blue eyes seeming afire. "The nun will have no problem picking you out of a lineup. But the fact the nun was kidnapped is the least of your worries."

"Kidnapped?" the man whispered, his face showing shock as he re-entered the conversation.

"I didn't kidnap anyone," Lupino announced. She looked into Ryan's eyes, silently pleading for him to take her side. The trap was getting tighter and more uncomfortable with each new revelation.

"We found heroin in that plane too," Meeker added. She glanced over to Ryan. "So if this is your girlfriend, you can add that to the list of her offenses as well."

"Grace," Ryan said, frowning in obvious confusion.

"She's wrong," a now panicking Lupino blabbered. But she knew her tone carried very little strength. The dynamic voice she was used to displaying on stage was now little more than a shrill whisper.

"Oh," Meeker continued, "there's also a matter of aiding and abetting a man wanted by the FBI for crimes including murder and espionage. Why don't you tell me about him? I'm betting Alistar Fister himself gave you this compact as a gift."

"Gal," Ryan asked, "who's this Fister guy?"

The singer said nothing. Like an animal caught in a cage, she sat silently, waiting for the trapper to make the next move.

"Grace Lupino," Meeker said, "you've got more trouble than you can imagine."

"If you have proof of anything you just said," Grace suggested, trying to make one last valiant protest, "why don't you arrest me?"

Meeker tossed the compact to Lupino as she stood. "Who said I was with the cops or the government? For the moment,

I'm just a woman who has something you lost. And it was found in a Cessna in Texas. By the way, the pilot of that plane is dead."

"But..."

The guest pointed the Colt at Lupino. "Don't talk, just listen. I'm here to tell you that you're being followed. We've been watching someone trail you for the past day. He doesn't look too friendly either. If I were you, I wouldn't want to be alone because that would give the boogieman a chance to move in. So if this is your boyfriend, you might want to keep him close by."

"Dick Diamond will protect me," Lupino announced, doing her best to stem her trembling.

"I wouldn't let him know anything about this," Meeker suggested as she slipped the gun back into her purse. "When he finds out what they can charge you with, he'll have to cut you loose. In the past, he had crime connections, and there are a host of law agencies that would love to tie him to kidnapping, the drug trade, or selling secrets to the enemy. Right now the D.A. in this city is very interested in putting Mr. Diamond behind bars. So if you want to hold onto your job, stay mute, songbird."

Meeker smiled, crossed the room, opened the door, and hurriedly left, unseen, through the back exit.

CHAPTER II

Tuesday, April 21, 1942
11:50 PM
Washington D.C.

Meeker had barely cleared the singer's dressing room when Spencer Ryan grabbed Lupino, yanking her off the couch and into his arms. As he held her protectively against his body, he demanded, "What's this all about?"

"I'm in trouble." She paused for a few seconds, as if trying to figure a way to skirt the truth while keeping the man's confidence. "That woman can trace me to a long list of things." She turned and looked into his eyes. "But I didn't do any of them. I made some bad choices in friends, and that put me in the wrong places at the wrong times. I've been set up, that's all."

"Who was she?"

"I'm guessing she works for a man I know. I've got something he wants."

"Who is this man?"

"He's scary, and he's everywhere. He's like an octopus; his tentacles can reach anywhere. He plays with people's lives and then kills them on whims."

They were getting close, and Ryan wasn't about to give up now. "Grace, who does he work for?"

She dug her face deeper into his chest. "I don't know. At times I think it might be the Germans, and at other times it seems like he's tied to the mob. I just don't know."

Ryan lifted his hands to her face and gently pulled upward until their eyes met. "How do you know him? What's his name?"

Her answer was rapid–fire. "I was a nobody, living in a backwoods town in Michigan, when he spotted me singing at a county fair. I was poor, hungry, and living in a home where my father beat me. He offered me a way out."

"How?"

"Not what you think," she assured him. "He gave me a new name, got me singing and charm lessons, bought me clothes, and got me jobs singing in clubs. He made me over into what he needed. The money was good, I liked the attention, and he never asked me for sex. There were times I had to run errands for him, but that was it. He told me it was best I never know what I was doing. He always said that the less I knew, the longer I'd live."

Ryan kept his voice gentle but firm, as he repeated the question. "What's his name?"

She shook her head, her sad eyes painting a picture of fear and surrender. "I'll never say. He told me if I ever whispered his name, I wouldn't live for an hour."

"He was just saying that," Ryan argued as he stroked her

THE DEVIL'S EYES *In the President's Service Series: Episode 5*

hair.

"Oh no," she replied, her tone hushed to the point he had to strain to hear her words. "I know it's true. I've seen five different people die who dared to say his name. He has eyes and ears everywhere. He'd know if I told you. Then not only would I be dead, but he'd have you killed too."

Ryan decided to switch tactics. "Grace, what about the document the woman asked you about?"

"I can't tell you about that either, but that's why I'm being followed. As long as he doesn't have the documents and I don't say his name, he won't do anything to me."

Her words hung in the air, frozen and cold. The woman was holding two cards, and they both appeared to be wild. It was obvious she wasn't going to reveal either one of them, at least not now.

"Do you want to get out of here?" Ryan asked, grasping at straws. "I've got a friend whose apartment isn't being used today. She's out of town. I have a key; we could go there and try to figure this thing out."

She sighed and nodded. "Yeah, that would be good."

"Do you need to go by your place and get some things?"

She once more pushed her face into his chest. She was shaking like a cold, wet, orphaned puppy.

"Not right now. I have enough things here to get me through the night. I'll just pack them up. But for now, I just want to be held."

Ryan couldn't help himself. He knew the woman in his arms was dangerous and deadly, but at this moment he still felt sorry for her and he did enjoy feeling her heart beating next to his.

CHAPTER 12

Wednesday, April 22, 1942
12:01 AM
Outside Springfield, Illinois

"You need me?" Alistar Fister asked as he walked into the large underground lab where, in a very real sense, he had been created and was now the key to his survival being refined.

Looking through a microscope, seemingly not hearing the visitor's question, was Fredrick Bauer. After several long moments, he pulled his eyes from the slide to his guest. He nodded as he announced, "My sources tell me we have a problem."

A shudder rushed through Fister's body as he took a quick inventory of his last few days. He'd done everything he'd been asked and had not as much as showed anything but respect to Bauer. He felt good too. The drug had seemingly stabilized his health. There had been no more seizures…at least none that he knew of. So what was this all about?

Bauer shut off the microscope, walked across the room, and took a seat in a wooden chair beside Emma's desk. After pushing his hands together in front of his face, he spoke. "I'm concerned that Grace Lupino might turn on us."

"Based on what she did to me, I think she already has."

"Yes, she did go rogue in the matter of the documents. But as far as I'm concerned, she wasn't doing anything more then than thinking on her feet. You had them, she knew you were on my hit list, and she saw the opportunity to get a piece of the action. I admire that."

Fister eased up on the corner of the desk and folded his arms. "So what's the problem?"

"She thinks I'm following her. That means she's likely getting nervous. She might just panic and flip on us."

"Can she prove anything?"

"Well, she was here once." Bauer glanced toward the stairs. "That could be a problem. But I can handle that. I was very careful on her visit, so while she can't really wound us, she can put us…" He glanced back to his lab table. "…under the microscope. And that would make our jobs a bit harder. I don't want that to happen."

Bauer shifted in the chair and dropped his hands to his side. Turning his gaze to his guest as if to refocus, he asked, "How do you feel?"

"Great," he assured his boss.

"Good. The last injection seemed to bring you back up to where you were before you were arrested by the FBI. And on

THE DEVIL'S EYES *In the President's Service Series: Episode 5*

this mission, I need you at full strength."

"Is it Grace?"

"I need you to eliminate her. Would you mind doing that?"

He shrugged. "It's just a job. Besides, I couldn't afford to let anything happen to you."

"Alistar, you're getting smarter. You now realize that anything that harms me kills you. In that sense, our hearts beat together. But remember this: my heart can go on without yours, but yours has to have mine."

Fister swallowed his irritation. "I know that. So do you know where Grace is?"

"She's on the run tonight. But when she starts to think clearly, she'll go back to her apartment. You can do the job there."

"If she's under pressure, why hasn't she already sold us out?"

"Because she knows she dies if she does."

"But what if they provide her with protection? What if they give her immunity? Couldn't she still cause your demise? She told me about the bodies buried behind the barn, and you admit she's seen you and is familiar with your operation. Considering what she knows, you don't seem very scared."

"Walk with me back to the house," Bauer suggested, not speaking again until they were seated in his study.

"Alistar," Bauer began as he propped his feet up on his desk, "there are no bodies anywhere on this farm. They can dig all they want to."

"But she said—"

"She said that because I took her to those places and told her they were there."

"You lied?"

He nodded. "It was necessary. I did it to convince her I had no conscious, and I could easily and without remorse kill anyone who crossed or disappointed me. She bought the story and understands the principle behind it."

"But she knows you," Fister pointed out.

"She knows an elderly farmer," he explained. "The one time she was here, I told her about secret labs but never actually showed them to her. I told her about you and the others, but she never saw any of you either. The man she spoke with was an old farmer with white hair and a beard. He was stooped and frail. He wore thick glasses and spoke with a lisp."

"How?"

"Make-up. If she talks, the man she'll describe is not the one the FBI will interview. What's even better, the picture she'll paint does perfectly describe the real Fredrick Bauer. That's the person who owned and farmed this place for years until he sold it to me and disappeared. Even the people in this area have never seen me enough to really identify me. And neither Grace nor you actually know my real name. So it won't matter what she says."

Fister nodded. "Then why do you want to bother taking her out?"

"Alistar, I can sense when a person is becoming disloyal by the way they act. They make the mistake of thinking they're free. She's forgotten she sold her soul to me and I own it. As owner, I also have the right to snuff it out. I will accept and even forgive a lot of things, but not disloyalty."

THE DEVIL'S EYES *In the President's Service Series: Episode 5*

Fister grimaced. He'd never known anyone like Bauer, or whatever his name really was. He was ruthless and smart. He had no real principles but had clear and precise goals. He was heartless and unforgiving, and yet he was still somehow very human. In fact, his charisma almost demanded people pay attention to him and give him their full devotion. When that charisma faded, it was replaced with merciless action. It was a lethal combination.

"Alistar," Bauer said, interrupting Fister's thoughts, "you did good work with Professor Williams. He has the funding, he's turned his classes over to a close friend in the department, and he's already digging through contacts and clues that will lead him to the grave we need to find. What I really admire more than his curiosity and drive is the fact that he has no problem using bribes to get what he wants. It's absolutely refreshing to deal with an academic man who so easily sets his integrity to one side."

"You believe he's onto something?"

"I believe he'll find the grave and the map," Bauer explained. "I don't believe the Indian woman who had her picture made forty years ago is the same one who met de Soto. But I don't have to believe it; I just have to convince Hitler it's true."

"And when he gets the map in his hands?"

"Then we'll find the well and we'll go into the bottled water business. Adolf will start drinking and expecting miracles. And because he has nothing but yes-men around him, he'll be told time and again how much younger he looks."

Fister couldn't suppress the flicker of hope that fueled his next question. "But what if it's real?"

Bauer shook his head and chuckled. "Alistar, my injections gave you a taste of being almost godlike, and now you love it so much you want to find some way to stay in that line of work forever. I'll admit, that sort of power is addicting." Pulling his feet off the desk and moving to the window, his voice became more subdued. "You will learn, if you haven't already, that, while we can kill our enemies, we can't rule the world. It's just too big. Those who somehow believe they can—and Hitler is one of them—always die and are buried by their own lustful desires." He turned and locked his eyes onto Fister. "So don't waste your time trying to dodge death; instead, find a way to have power as you live. You've heard my plan and you likely can begin to realize that my vision can succeed. And here's the important part. Unlike some despot who wants to gobble up land and rule scores or even millions of people, I'll let others have all the property they want and make any law they desire." He paused and smiled. "What I want is to own their souls. That's where the real power is. When they surrender to the products I tempt them with, they'll be mine."

Suddenly Fister understood Bauer was a devil, maybe not the one who tempted Christ, but his goals were the same. Without even knowing it, Fister had sold his soul to this man, exactly as Grace Lupino and countless others had done. And it was impossible to get his soul back from the person who was keeping him alive.

"Alistar," his host announced as he once more took a seat behind his desk, "you might want to resurrect your identity as

THE DEVIL'S EYES *In the President's Service Series: Episode 5*

O'Malley. That'll give you a cover. And as there are people in Washington who've met you, I'd suggest you add a beard and glasses to further disguise your look. Ask Emma to give you a make-up kit." He paused. "And don't kill Grace until you get the documents. I can't afford to have those things out where anyone might find them. Check the information desk when you arrive at the Washington train station. Your final instructions will be there."

"Where do I go when the job is finished?"

"I'll likely be away, digging up some information I need, but you can come back here. But don't lose the package this time. That's what created this whole mess anyway, where greed trumped logic. By the way, how did she find out about the package? Did you tell her?"

Fister shook his head. "I thought you did."

"Okay, now something else makes sense. My source tells me a man has been following her. I doubt if she's picked up on it yet. He might be after the package as well."

"Any idea who he is?"

"No," Bauer admitted. "But keep your eye out for him as well. If he grabs the documents before you can get them, the mission includes taking him out too. I have to have that package. My credibility depends upon it."

"So I'm going to take out the songbird, as you called her, get the package, and find out who tipped Lupino off that I had the materials."

Bauer nodded. "And bring them back to me, which means getting back here alive."

No more words were said nor needed. Fister fully understood his mission and at least a part of why it was vital. And as Grace Lupino had already sold him out, he had a score to settle, so this job would be a sweet one. Not only would he eliminate her, but he would also make sure the woman suffered in ways she couldn't begin to imagine.

CHAPTER 13

Thursday, April 22, 1942
8:43 AM
Washington D.C.

Spencer Ryan stood in the undersized kitchen of the small, one-bedroom apartment that had been Becca Bobbs' before the team formed and she supposedly died in a plane crash. As he leaned against the counter of the white metal cabinets, he heard stirrings in the bedroom. The woman he'd theoretically rescued the night before, at least in her mind, was evidently now awake. A few moments later his theory was proven correct as Grace Lupino, not surprisingly wrapped in a red robe, strolled out into the living room. Her hair was a mess and her manner unsure.

"Good morning," Ryan said. "Did you sleep well?"

"Not really. How about you?"

"I've spent the night on worse couches."

"I kind of expected you to come in with me," she said, her dark eyes almost as lifeless as her defeated tone.

"I'm first and foremost a gentleman. I save damsels in distress, not take advantage of them when they're weak. If I did, they'd kick me out of the knight's union."

A faint smile flickered across her face as she sat down at the tiny dinette table. "You're the first man I've ever met who thought that way. I just believed it was written into the rules of the game that when you brought a woman home for the night, you expected payment."

As he studied her face, unadorned with make-up, he noted a childlike quality. For a moment Lupino looked like the little girl who'd fallen off her bike and skinned her knee. Yet this was no little girl, and her wounds were much deeper and harder to address than a scratched leg.

"Grace, you want something to eat?"

"I told you, my friends call me Gal. At this point, you've more than earned the friend title."

"Okay, Gal, I slipped down to a corner store and got a few things. How about some scrambled eggs?"

She pointed to the chair. "Not yet. I'd rather you'd sit down with me and have a talk."

Ryan moved to the table, pulled out the chrome chair, and took a seat. "I'm sitting. Now what?"

"How much of what you told me the night before last was true?"

He blushed. "Not much of it."

"Didn't think so. But even though I knew you were lying, I sensed you weren't on the make. That made you kind of sweet in my mind. And last night you rose to the level of Sir Galahad."

A seasoned operative would have brushed that comment off like lint from a suit, but the doctor was too new to this game. The fact he was just playing a part in order to gain information suddenly caused a wave of guilt to crash over him. Within seconds, he'd almost drowned in the backwash.

"What's wrong?" she asked. "You look kind of down."

"I'm just not as noble as you think I am."

She grinned. "But you sure know how to give a girl a great hug."

"That comes natural."

"Jim, I've dragged you into a mess. My life's not worth a plug nickel. I'm going to die as sure as the sun comes up each morning, and it's not going to be from old age. You break as many rules as I've broken and they start to wager on you expiring in weeks, not years."

"We all die."

"I know. And I got to thinking last night, as I tried and failed to go to sleep, that death might actually be a relief." She let her eyes meet his before continuing. "I wasn't really honest either, at least not with that woman who barged into my dressing room. I knew what I was getting into. In fact, I set it up. The man who gave me the compact is working against the Allies. I didn't know it when he gave it to me a month or so ago, but I knew it when I went to Texas. I also knew he had something I wanted, something of great value, and I went down there to steal it. I thought I was smart enough to use what he had to buy back my soul."

"Your soul?"

"Yeah, my soul."

"Who's the guy you met in Texas?"

"Alistar Fister. I'm only telling you this because the last time I saw him he was all but dead. So he can't hurt me or you anymore."

If she was right and Fister was dead, then at least one good thing had come out of this affair. Talking a deep breath, he tried to reassure her. "Then if this guy's dead, it's going to be okay. The man with reasons to kill you can't hurt you anymore."

She sighed. "No. It'll never be okay. Fister was the least of my worries. He fell for my charms, and he was easy to control. It doesn't make any difference if he's dead or not, at least not in this matter. But I'm not mourning his death. In fact, I hope it wasn't just painful but humiliating."

Ryan shouldn't have been, but he was shocked at the woman's suddenly cold, calculating reaction to Fister's demise. The look on her face told him she'd somehow gotten a morbid sense of pleasure from the thought of the man in pain. Her next line left him frozen.

"I know what it's like to die because I've killed people. They weren't good people, but they were people. I knew when I snuffed the life out of them that somewhere they likely had someone who loved them. Yet I blew them out like a candle. I did it because I was told to. And until last night, I never lost any sleep over it either. Then last night, their death rattles came back to haunt me."

The thought of killing another person was so foreign to Ryan he had problems comprehending it. His calling was in saving lives, not taking them. Yet this small woman, with pure ivory skin and a voice that could charm birds out of trees, was also a murderer. She talked about it as matter-of-factly as if she were reciting a shopping list.

"What would have happened if you hadn't followed orders?" he asked, his eyes catching hers and holding on.

"I wouldn't have gotten my apartment, or my job, or the money I've got in the bank. I would also have been killed. In other words, I'd have been dead and buried long ago."

"So it was either they die or you do."

"If it were only that simple. I killed in cold blood, and that's how I'll die too. Jim, I didn't care about those people I killed. Some of them I'd kissed, held in my arms, whispered sweet nothings in their ear, and then pushed a knife into their hearts. I had no regrets. None! Until now. But I think my sudden remorse is only because I'm trapped, and right now someone has likely already ordered my execution."

She shook her head and looked toward the window. "I'm not just another woman sitting at this table; I'm a monster."

"But—"

She held up her hand and smiled. "It's true. And for the moment, this monster is not going to die. You know why?"

Ryan shook his head.

"Because they won't act on my writ of execution until they know where the package is. That secret keeps me alive." She laughed. "Usually people take secrets to their graves, but I have one that will keep the grave waiting."

"I guess that's good."

"But there's one thing that bothers me."

"What?"

"How does anyone know that I have it?" Her face framed in a look of confusion. "He should have thought it went down with the—"

"Went down with what?"

"Nothing," she said, her finger tracing her lips. "He must be alive. He told him."

"Who told who?" the doctor demanded.

"I just figured out something I should have done. I thought my plan was foolproof. I thought he'd die, but he didn't. He must have gotten back to the base."

"I'm not following you."

She shook her head. "It still doesn't matter. Maybe it's better that he knows I got it. If he does, then I'm actually in pretty good shape. I was a fool to let that floozy who invaded my dressing room scare me." Lupino smiled. "That was stupid. After all, I still hold a winning hand."

Ryan nodded. This was all about the package. And while he was almost sure he knew what was in the illusive cardboard tube, he had to play dumb, but he also had to keep her talking. If she continued to think out loud long enough, she might slip.

"You sure it's safe?"

"No one knows where it is."

Sensing she didn't trust him enough to share the location and not wanting to appear too pushy, Ryan again took the conversation in a different direction. "What about the guy giving the orders? Who's he?"

"Just an old man with lots of power."

"Where is he? Maybe we could take him out."

"He's usually in the Midwest—Illinois, to be precise. He's bent, white-haired, wears thick glasses, and dresses like a hick. But looks can be deceiving. In the matter of real power, he has more than anyone I know. He's a brilliant scientist."

"He doesn't sound too scary. Where in Illinois can we find him?"

"I don't know," she admitted. "The only time I was there I was blindfolded on the trip in and the trip out. But that doesn't matter, at least not right now. I have to go back to my apartment."

"But he'll know you're there. And so will that woman who visited your dressing room."

Without a word, Lupino rose and moved back toward the bedroom. Just before entering, she turned and said, "As long as I possess what he wants, he won't kill me." She paused, pushing a strand of black hair from her face before adding, "And you don't ever need to see me again. If he finds you with me, he'd kill you in a New York minute, and you don't have enough time left to waste a minute on me." She sighed. "I'm getting soft. It seems I actually care if someone lives or dies."

As Ryan watched the bedroom door close behind her, he took stock of her final words. She was writing him off, not because he didn't measure up to her standards, but because he far exceeded them. And at this moment, even knowing all he knew about her, he still yearned to play Sir Galahad at least one more time.

CHAPTER 14

Friday, April 23, 1942
2:32 AM
Pleasant Grove Cemetery, Saratoga Springs, New York

The fact the night was overcast served Bauer almost as well as did the fresh grave's soft dirt. It took his two mute henchmen just thirty minutes of digging to reach the coffin. They brushed away the last bit of soil from the lid before looking up for instructions.

"You," he said, pointing to the larger of the two men, "pry it open. And, Bill, you get out of the hole and stand by me."

As one scrambled from the grave and the other went to work getting the container's lid loose, Bauer glanced around the large deserted graveyard. Though a bit rolling, Pleasant Grove was easy to navigate and rather picturesque. If one had to spend eternity somewhere, this place had charm. Trees lined the walks and the cemetery's main road. As they had made their way across the grounds to Helen Meeker's final resting spot, he'd noted graves predating the Revolutionary war. In other places, there were six and seven generations of one family buried together. Some of the older stones had epitaphs that were dead serious. His favorite was, "William was a rogue who worked little and drank much. Thus his finally destination will leave him well out of touch." Another was just as humorous but far less ominous: "All things considered I'd rather be in Cleveland."

Glancing to his left he noted a large crypt at the top of a rise. On this cloudy night, that expensive final resting place looked ominous and foreboding, yet it still toyed with his curiosity. He yearned to make the fifty-yard walk to read the family name and find out the date the structure was built. It was all he could do to hold his ground. But for the moment his focus had to be on the business at hand. He needed to look into the casket, find out who was spending eternity in that grave, and then have his men return the plot to its original condition.

Looking down into the hole, Bauer watched the man struggle. He knelt on the bottom part of the box and used a small crowbar to pry loose the top lid. The high-dollar coffin was not giving up easily.

"Why not just a pine box?" Bauer complained. "Why do people spend so much money on something that'll never be seen?"

The man next to him peered into the hole and shrugged.

"We need to get moving," Bauer urged the big man. "Can't afford to get caught."

Finally, as the larger of the two mutes put his full weight

THE DEVIL'S EYES *In the President's Service Series: Episode 5*

into it, the bar made some headway. First there was a groan, then the sound of a hinge snapping, and finally the long creaking moan when the viewing panel was pulled open.

It was time. Bauer yanked a flashlight from his dark overcoat. Walking over to the grave's head, he pushed the switch on the light but nothing happened. He repeated his effort five or six more times with the same results. Unscrewing the lens, he looked inside. Nothing appeared out of place. As he poured the trio of batteries out into his gloved hand, he noticed one of them was leaking. He cursed, grabbed the faulty electrical cylinder, and tossed it toward the crypt up the hill. While it fell well short of its target, it did manage to make a long pinging sound as it struck a granite marker. After dropping the other batteries back into the flashlight and retightening the top, he shoved it into his coat pocket and looked back at the grave. There was simply too little light to see anything. Now the cloudy sky was working against him.

"Get out," Bauer ordered the man standing on the casket.

The worker immediately pulled himself from the hole. As he dusted himself off, Bauer yanked off his coat, handing it to the smaller of his two men, pushed through the freshly piled dirt, and moved to the grave's edge. First he sat with his legs dangling into the hole and then dropped down to the coffin, his leather heels making a dull clanking noise as he landed on the lid. Steadying himself, he eased to his knees and looked into the casket. It was still too dark to see anything.

After muttering another oath, he reached past the lid with

his right hand and felt for the body. What he found was nothing more than an empty pillow resting on satin lining. He pushed his hand down. There was nothing there. The box was empty.

"I told you," a woman's voice cried out. "I told you I'm still alive."

Bauer bolted upright, pushed to his feet, and as if the hounds of hell were chasing him, leapt from the grave. His eyes as large as saucers, he glanced past the mute and now mystified men.

"Where are you?"

"You have to find me," the voice answered.

Pushing his gloved hand through his hair, he whirled and looked back into the grave. He knew it was empty, but where was the voice coming from? Was it really his Gretchen calling out to him, or was he making that slow descent into the madness that had consumed his father so many years before?

CHAPTER 15

Friday, April 23, 1942
1:15 PM
Outside Drury, Maryland

Meeker looked at her notes, trying to put together the few pieces she had to make sense of a much larger puzzle. As she studied her words, she hoped an idea would magically come to her. When it didn't, she stalked from the library table to the window. Glancing out on the Maryland countryside, she took a deep breath and considered the scant facts she knew.

If she were trying to hide something where no one would find it but where it would still be safe, where would she put it? Over the years of working first with the FBI, next the Secret Service, and finally the OSS, she'd learned the best hiding places were usually the most obvious. When she'd solved the case of the yellow Packard, the money had been hidden in a car seat. How many times had people sat on that seat without anyone guessing an eccentric old woman had stashed her fortune there? In that case, figuring the "where" had taken years, and she didn't have years right now. Besides, in this case, the car was out. Grace Lupino didn't even own a car. When she needed one, she borrowed her boss's Chevy. And she wouldn't put two of the world's most important documents where Dick Diamond might happen onto them. Hence, the only chance at uncovering the package was to get inside the woman's head, and the songbird at The Grove was not easy to break.

Based on what Meeker had learned from Spencer Ryan, Lupino was a careful woman who valued control at the very same time her own life seemed to be spiraling out of control. Thus, logic said the singer would have chosen a spot close to home. But where? Meeker had searched the entertainer's dressing room while Lupino was singing, and there was nothing of importance there. Ryan assured her the singer had taken nothing that could hold the documents with her to Bobbs' old apartment. That left the woman's apartment as the only logical choice. But would a woman who seemed to cover her tracks as well as Lupino place something of great value — perhaps even the key to her living or dying — in such an obvious location?

"We're back," Reese announced as he and Bobbs entered the room.

"And?" Meeker turned to face the pair of seasoned investigators.

It was the man in the dark blue suit that spoke first. "Lupino left her apartment about nine. Becca tailed her."

The blonde took up the story. "She went to three different clothing stores, where she looked at several red outfits but bought nothing. She stopped at Walgreens and had coffee in a back

THE DEVIL'S EYES *In the President's Service Series: Episode 5*

booth. She takes it without sugar. Next she went to Darnell's Beauty Shop. Based on what I observed, black is not her natural color. She then caught a cab and returned home."

"While Becca was following Lupino," Reese explained, "I got into her apartment and carefully went through the place. In fact, I was so careful she'll never know anyone was there. I looked in, under, and over everything. When I finished, I did it again. There's nothing there. I even checked for hidden wall safes and secret panels. If the documents are hidden in her apartment, then she's outwitted me. I didn't see them anywhere."

Meeker shrugged. "If not the apartment, then where?"

"There was something else that proved interesting," Bobbs suggested.

"What's that?" Meeker asked.

"I wasn't the only one tailing her," the blonde explained. "There was a man, likely in his late thirties, wearing a gray tweed sports coat and dark slacks, that shadowed her every move. Based on his face, he'd been doing it for a while. He needed a shave. He was still watching her as she returned to her apartment."

"I thought I recognized him from where I was waiting in our car," Reese chimed in. "So I stepped out and got close enough to make a positive I.D. His name is Paul 'Rocko'" Wells. He's a private investigator whose clients often walk on the wrong side of the legal tracks. He's more than a bit slimy, but he knows his business."

"So," Meeker asked, "why would someone pay Wells to keep tabs on Lupino? According to what the woman told Spencer, the only way the cat got out of the bag was that Fister must have made it back to the boss. Unless…"

Bobbs smiled. "Are you back to thinking Alistar's working for organized crime and they're calling the shots?"

"It's always made sense to me."

"I think we need to work over Rocko," Reese suggested. "If I used enough of the third degree, I could likely get him to talk."

"You're supposed to be dead," the team leader noted. "We can't blow that cover on a wild hunch that might lead nowhere." As the two followed her movements, Meeker returned to the library table and studied her notes. Turning to Reese, she posed a cryptic question. "What about Reggie?"

"I'm not seeing where you're heading," the agent replied.

"If Rocko Wells is working for the unknown big boss, then he'd likely know Fister. Why don't you arrange for Reggie to go see the gumshoe? If Wells doesn't know who Fister is, then we can be pretty sure we have a second player in this game. I mean, based on what Spencer found out, it wouldn't be out of the question for Lupino to have a long list of people who want to see the songbird stopped in mid-note. She's admitted to several murders."

"I can get moving on Rocko," Reese assured her. "But what about Lupino?"

"Is Barnes watching her right now?" Meeker asked.

"Yeah."

"We have her covered then, so you find a way for Wells and Reggie to come face to face."

As Reese hurried from the room, the team leader turned her

attention to Bobbs. "What do know about controlled fires?"

"You mean, like the forest service uses or the ones that are a part of movie magic? They call those special effects."

Meeker looked her friend in the eye. "The latter."

"Helen, what do you have in mind?"

"Lupino is still working. She's going to the club every night. While she's gone, can you put together something in her apartment that'll create enough smoke to make her think the place is on fire without really burning anything down?"

Bobbs grinned. "That wouldn't be hard. What's your goal in all of this?"

"I'll be there waiting for her. When the fire starts, my guess is, if the documents are there, she'll save them."

"But Henry looked everywhere."

Meeker folded her arms and smiled. "I have no doubt Henry would've found the documents if a man had hidden them. But we both know women are much better at hiding things than our male counterparts. I mean, who did a better job hiding Christmas and birthday presents at your house?"

"My mother. I could never find where she put them."

"Exactly. It's time we smoke out Lupino."

"And if the documents aren't there?"

"Then we'll know that fact for sure, and we'll have put another scare into the woman her friends know as Gal. I want her scared again."

"When are we going to do it?"

"Tomorrow. That'll give you plenty of time to get what you need for the job."

CHAPTER 16

Friday, April 23, 1942
4:30 PM
Washington D.C.

There was something about American automobiles that Reggie Fister loved. It was more than their power and smooth ride; it was their design. It seemed Detroit produced cars that not only went from point A to point B quickly, but they made the trip in style. The long black 1937 Buick Henry Reese had picked from their fleet for the trip to Washington was a perfect example of the Yanks' overstated love of large and excessive motorcars. The pontoon front fenders were fat, round, and stretched five feet or more from the waterfall grill to the front doors. The passenger compartment was so massive it could have been a venue for a high school dance. And then there was the car's nose.

"My goodness," Fister exclaimed, "this has to be the longest bonnet I've ever seen!"

"Bonnet?" a confused Reese asked as he pulled the Buick up

to the curb and switched off the eight-cylinder motor.

The Scotsman laughed. "I mean, the hood. Even with the steering wheel on the wrong side, I forgot where I was for a moment."

"A straight-eight is a long engine," the agent said with a shrug. "Now, enough about the car. If you'll look up to the street corner, a half-block down, right by that Alexander Street sign, you'll spot the man you need to meet. That's Paul 'Rocko' Wells, leaning against the same lamppost he was holding up earlier in the day. His eyes are directed toward Grace Lupino's apartment building. So he's still on the case."

As his eyes honed in on the target, Reggie Fister leaned forward and peered out the Buick's split windshield and across a hood that seemed to stretch halfway to Maryland. Once he'd taken full stock of the layout, he noted, "Looks like he's gone a few rounds in a boxing ring."

"And didn't cover up too well," Reese cracked. "Still, looks can be deceiving. While he appears dimwitted, he's crafty as a fox and a lot quicker than most athletes. He's so careful and covers his tracks so well that in his decade or more of doing clandestine jobs for the underworld, the FBI and other law enforcement agencies have never been able to pin a jaywalking charge on the guy."

Fister nodded. "Well, all I have to do is stroll up and say a big cheerio and see if he responds. So my beating him in a footrace down the block isn't a needed skill at this moment."

"Exactly," the agent answered while turning to face his passenger. "You might have to poke him a bit to unnerve the big

THE DEVIL'S EYES *In the President's Service Series: Episode 5*

guy."

"What do you mean by that?"

"I mean, you might have to visit for a while, keep pushing, try to get him to respond in such a way that we're sure he's not just staying off the radar because that's what he was told to do. In other words, he and your brother might have an agreement to not recognize each other in public."

"Got it. Anything more I need to know?"

"Nope."

"Well, as you Yanks say, here goes nothing."

Fister pulled up the handle and swung the heavy door open. Stepping from the car, he gazed up into a nickel-gray sky before taking stock of what was around him. It was a typical Saturday in a mostly residential neighborhood. People walked up and down the sidewalk, a few stopped in at the drugstore, and some lingered on street corners chatting. Like almost everywhere else he visited in America, most of them constantly checked their watches as if that would either speed time up or slow it down.

Shoving his hands into his gray pants pockets, the Scotsman walked a dozen steps before stepping between two cars that were parallel-parked in front of a brick home. After glancing both ways and waiting for a Yellow cab to pass, he crossed the street. Turning right on the walk, he ambled along until he was within ten feet of Rocko Wells. Stopping, he casually studied the man's pock-marked face, deep heavy brow, jutting jaw, foreboding eyes, and thick lips. As Fister expected, it took the detective only a few seconds to realize he was being observed.

"What's your problem?" Wells snapped.

Fister covered the ground between himself and the private investigator before replying. "I know you."

"Is that so?" Wells barked. "Well, good for you. Go into the store, tell them that, and maybe they'll give you a cigar."

Foster wasn't put off by the crass response. Instead he grinned and good-naturedly explained, "Wouldn't do me any good; I don't smoke. Now, let me ask you again; what's your name?"

"What's it to you?"

"I just thought if I heard it, I might know where we've met."

Wells glanced from his uninvited guest to the apartment and back. "It's Wells. My friends call me Rocko, but you aren't one of my friends, so move on."

"Mine's Fister."

"I don't remember asking, and I don't care." Wells stepped forward, his face all but pressing into the Scotsman's nose. "I'm not looking for friends, but I wouldn't mind making another enemy. Now get out of here or you'll find yourself seeing stars… if you get my drift."

Fister stepped back and shrugged. "Just believed we'd met somewhere. Guess I was wrong." He paused. "You know, I think my boss mentioned your name to me yesterday."

"Your boss?" Wells' tone was now a bit more relaxed.

"The man who put you on this job." When Wells didn't immediately respond, the Scotsman kept pushing. "I know you're watching Grace. I was just checking up to make sure you were doing your job. After all, we're paying you well for it."

Wells seemed to consider what he'd heard before lowering his voice and leaning closer. This time he showed no hint of

THE DEVIL'S EYES *In the President's Service Series: Episode 5*

aggressiveness.

"You said your name was Fister?"

"Yeah. Does it mean anything to you?"

"No, but you mean a lot if you work with Lucky."

"You said it."

"Okay, you tell him I'm getting close. I'll have his bargaining chips within a couple of days. The songbird hasn't sung yet, but she will. You got that?"

The Scotsman raised his eyebrows and nodded. Saying nothing, he pivoted and walked back toward the Buick. Knowing Wells' eyes were following his every move, he didn't stop until he was a half-block past and around a corner from where Reese sat in the car. He casually stood there, watching an old man feed peanuts to a squirrel, until the agent pulled the Buick around the block. After making sure Wells couldn't see him, Fister opened the door and slid inside.

"Did he know you?" Reese asked.

"No. But I did convince him I worked for his boss and I was there checking up on the job he was doing."

"Nice move. For a Brit, you have some good instincts."

"I'm from Scotland," Fister corrected him. "Wells is working for somebody named Lucky. And Grace Lupino has a couple of things Lucky needs for bargaining chips. Does that mean anything to you?"

"Yeah," Reese replied with a grim smile. "If it means what I think it means, Wells is being paid by a man looking for a free pass out of jail. Let's get back to the headquarters and share what we know with Helen."

CHAPTER 17

Friday, April 23, 1942
8:30 PM
Washington D.C.

Bauer parked five blocks from the Washington Memorial and walked aimlessly for fifteen minutes before finally ducking into a small coffee shop. He waited in a back booth, sipping on a hot cup of coffee, as he considered what he saw as an incredibly perplexing situation. Fister had seen Clay Barnes in Brownsville, Texas, and Meeker's grave in Saratoga Springs, New York, was empty. On top of that, there were no eyewitnesses to the plane crash that had supposedly killed both the Secret Service agent and the assistant to the president. And why was such a unique cast of characters with them on that flight? Where were they going, and why was it so important they were together on a private plane during a time of war? Things simply didn't add up. But was that a good enough reason for him to make the rash decision to visit a city he had always avoided? Even though no one knew him in the capitol, could he really afford to be seen… especially in the company of the man he was about to meet?

Shifting his gaze from the cup of coffee he was nursing to an army private at the counter, Bauer watched the slightly built soldier work on a ham sandwich. The green kid couldn't have been out of his teens, and he was obviously nervous. After taking a long sip from a six-ounce bottle of Coca-Cola, the young man reached into his pocket, pulled out some change, and headed to the jukebox. Leaning against the stained glass-and-wooden cabinet, he glanced through the unit's twenty selections before making his choice. Dropping a nickel into the slot, he hit a couple of buttons and then walked back to his stool. By the time he was seated, the strains of Glen Miller's hit single *Don't Sit Under the Apple Tree* filled the small room. As the G.I. listened to the words, he pulled out a wallet and studied a photograph. The kid was likely both homesick and lovesick, and neither of those maladies was going to be cured for a very long time.

Out of the corner of his eye, Bauer saw the eatery's front door open and James Killpatrick enter. The FBI agent glanced around the room for a moment, and after spotting Bauer, strolled confidently to the booth.

"Have a seat, Jimmy."

"This beats the stockyards," Killpatrick announced as he scooted onto the bench. After he was seated, an older, gray-haired waitress, wearing a light green dress and a stained white apron, walked over.

"What can I get you?" she asked.

"Coffee and a piece of cherry pie."

THE DEVIL'S EYES *In the President's Service Series: Episode 5*

"We've only got apple tonight. Is that okay?"

"That's fine." After she moved away, Killpatrick turned his attention to Bauer. "What are you looking at?"

"That young soldier," Bauer said, leaning his head toward the joint's main counter. "He picked that song on the jukebox and has been studying a photo in his wallet ever since. I bet he's wondering if his sweetheart will wait for him."

"And," the agent noted, "that girl is probably wondering if the kid will fall for a British gal."

"Maybe you're right." Bauer turned his gaze back to the agent. "You ever been in love…I mean, really in love?"

"No time for it. Dames, even good ones, get in the way of things. They cause us to lose our focus. Some even drive us crazy."

The tall man took a sip of coffee and nodded. Killpatrick might be closer to the truth than he could imagine, but now was not the time and this was likely not the person to discuss that troubling aspect of life with. In fact, with the waitress headed back to their table carrying the agent's order, now was not the time to discuss anything. The men remained silent until Killpatrick gobbled up his pie. After he'd wiped his mouth with a napkin, the agent broke the silence.

"What about you?"

Bauer frowned. "What do you mean?"

"You ever been in love?"

His heart twisted. "I have, but it was a long time ago."

"What happened?" Killpatrick picked up his coffee cup and took a long drink.

"I think she died."

"You *think*?"

"I mean, I know she died, but there are times when it feels like she's still here. There are moments I hear her voice, times I even think I see her." Suddenly Bauer wished he'd never brought up the subject. It was causing him to think too little and say too much.

"Must have been some kind of woman," the agent commented.

"Yes, but that's not why we're here. I trust you have agents assigned to track down the microfilm."

Killpatrick set his cup back on the wooden tabletop. "We're working on it, but no success so far. Do you think the Nazis have it?"

"They don't," Bauer assured his guest. "They're as lost as you are."

"That's a relief."

"I'm sure it is," Bauer replied with a smile, "but there are a couple of other things you might be interested in looking into."

"What's that?" Perhaps it was the time of the day or the location, but this time the agent seemed relaxed and unhurried.

"My sources spotted Clay Barnes in south Texas a couple of weeks ago."

"That's impossible. He's dead. They likely spotted someone who looked like him."

"No, it was him."

"A dead man walking?"

"Jimmy, do you suppose he was the mole at the White House, and Hoover or someone in the Secret Service was ordered to take him out? They planned the plane crash, but somehow Barnes got wind of it and missed the flight. So now the White House believes the traitor to be dead, when in fact he isn't."

"Interesting theory," Killpatrick said with a shrug, "but I'd still bet on mistaken identity."

"What would you say if I told you I don't believe there's a body in Helen Meeker's grave?"

The man's eyebrows shot up. "Is that why you asked about her during our last meeting?"

"My sources tell me that both Barnes and Meeker are still alive. If they are, then everyone in that plane crash is likely alive as well. And if that's true, what's this all about? Were all of them working for the Nazis? And when word got out, did they use the plane crash as a way of escaping? No one looks for dead people, especially those whose obituaries have been written and graves have been filled in."

"That makes no sense at all." Killpatrick looked skeptical as he waved his hand in dismissal. "The fact there's no one in Meeker's grave would mean the U.S. government would know she's not dead, so they wouldn't have announced her death. They'd have a nationwide manhunt going on right now, and I can assure you that's not happening because I'd be leading that investigation."

"So the empty grave doesn't bother you."

"How can you be sure it's empty?"

"Just my sources."

"If it really is, it just likely means there wasn't enough of her body found at the crash scene to bury."

Bauer nodded. "That's logical, but there's so much talk going on in Nazi circles about this that I think it would be worth your time to check it out."

"I'll put out a few queries," the agent assured him, "but they'll just be laughed off. Is there anything else?"

"Not tonight, but I'll be in touch. And I'll pay the bill."

"Thank you, but if we keep meeting like this, I need to have some kind of name to call you. Any suggestions?"

"Mr. Y."

"Why not Mr. X?" Killpatrick quipped.

"It's already been taken. Good night, Jimmy."

"Good night, Mr. Y."

Bauer watched the agent walk out the door before turning his attention back to the G.I. The kid had returned to the Wurlitzer and dropped another nickel into the slot. A few seconds later, the room filled with the sounds of Jimmy Dorsey's *Green Eyes*. Bauer frowned as he shared in the young man's misery.

CHAPTER 18

Friday, April 23, 1942
10:00 PM
Washington D.C.

Becca Bobbs and Clay Barnes sat in the blue 1939 Packard sedan parked opposite Lupino's apartment building and watched the all but vacant street. Barnes had been here most of the day, but Bobbs only joined him after completing her work in the lab. He couldn't deny, even to himself, that he was pleased when she showed up.

"That Rocko is a character," the woman noted. "That must be the fifteenth cigarette's he's lit since I got here."

"He'd already smoked a couple of packs before that too," the agent noted.

"You watched him close enough to know his brand?"

"Camels. And if you believe their ads, more doctors smoke Camels than any other brand because they're good for your throat."

Bobbs shrugged. "The advertising industry pitches everything as healthy." She studied the 1940 La Salle for a few moments. "So do you think he's working for Lucky Luciano?"

"Makes sense. Lucky's looking for a way out of prison. If he's found out about the documents Lupino has in her possession and he can get his hands on them, they'd be a huge bargaining chip for him."

"Guess so. He might go from being locked in prison to getting the key to Washington D.C. within minutes." She settled back into the seat. "Clay, you think it would be okay if I turned the radio on?"

"Keep the volume down and our windows up, and I believe it'd be fine."

She turned the knob and waited for the tubes to warm up. Thirty seconds later, the familiar strains of a door in bad need of oiling brought an immediate smile to her face.

"*Inner Sanctum,*" Barnes cracked, questioning her choice in programming. "I mean, why, when we're risking our lives on a stakeout, do you want to listen to something that deals with stuff like ax murderers and ghosts?"

"Aren't we ghosts? The world has mourned us, we're presumed dead, and yet we're still walking around. So in my mind, *Inner Sanctum* isn't about fantasy; it's all about the reality I live in."

"That's a pleasant thought. But don't you think the host… what's his name?"

"Raymond."

"Yeah, Raymond. His puns are horrible, and does anyone

really use the Carter's Little Liver Pills that sponsor this badly written trash masquerading as entertainment?"

"Only people with small livers use Carter's," Bobbs said with a grin. When Barnes didn't reply she frowned. "It was a pun. Didn't you get it when I said small?"

"Oh, I got it, but it was hardly a joke. It was almost as bad a pun as what I've heard on the show. Can't we listen to music instead?"

"Fine. Makes sense that a man who's scared of nuns gets nightmares from listening to a radio show."

"That was uncalled for."

"Really?"

"Yes. Big Bob Bobbs' daughter Becca Bobbs should know better."

"None of that."

He sat up straight. "Shut up," he ordered.

"I beg your pardon!"

"Wells is out of his car and coming this way. Shut up and kiss me."

He didn't give her time to catch her breath before grabbing her, drawing her into his arms, and placing his lips on hers. As they broke for an instant, he asked, "Is he still headed this way?"

"Who cares?" she whispered, bringing their lips together again.

CHAPTER 19

Saturday, April 24, 1942
1:04 PM
Conway, Arkansas

Professor Warren Williams sat on a threadbare couch in the tiny living room of a home located on the wrong side of the small Central Arkansas community's tracks. A few feet to his right an elderly woman, her dark face heavily lined with wrinkles but not a hint of gray in her long, black straight hair, was knitting while sitting in a wooden rocking chair. As she did her handwork, her dark eyes glowed.

"Thank you for allowing me into your home," Williams said.

"So you're here about Kawutz," she said without turning her head in his direction.

"I am."

"It's been a long time since her name's been spoken by anyone I know."

"She was once a legend."

The slightly built woman shook her head. "Legends are now baseball players. The young have no regard for the past. They've lost touch with the old ways. Most children today can't ride a pony or track a rabbit, much less speak our language."

The irony of his host feeling this way while living in the middle of a community built by non-Indians amused the professor, but he wasn't about to show it. This woman, now known as Sue, was the daughter of a Caddo chief. She had heard the stories that were never written down and had once known the mysterious woman at the center of the man's passion.

"She lived a long time," Williams noted.

"Her spirit walked on this earth for generations," Sue explained, her voice filled with great reverence. "Her spirit still walks in places."

"I've been told you buried her."

"I was there."

The woman finally turned her face to his. "She was buried with the things that were important to her. That's how it should be." She studied him for a moment. "Why are you so interested? This is of no concern to your race."

"I'm a professor of history. I feel her story needs to be told and her legend needs to be known."

She shook her head. "I'm old enough to remember thousands of things your people told my people that weren't true. You took us from our land and moved us to places with no value. Our stories were lost because your people deemed them unworthy of remembering. Our children now know nothing about the proud lives their ancestors once lived. To this day, we are looked at as mindless savages. Why should I believe you came into my home to do anything but tell more lies?"

"I will not dispute your words," Williams replied, his eyes locking onto hers. "But that's not the way I feel. I'm ashamed of what my people have done to yours. I mourn what's been lost. My tears fall for children who have no contact with their culture."

Sue silently studied the visitor's face a while longer. As Williams had no way of knowing what she was thinking, he felt like a defendant in a murder trial, waiting for the judge to render his verdict. Finally, after she looked back toward the wall and folded her hands in her lap, she spoke. "She still walks in the government-owned land on the mountain overlooking the river. There is where she met the Frenchman, and her spirit waits for his return. He was her one true love."

"Are you saying she's buried there?"

She turned back to once more stare deeply into his eyes. "The body and spirit are never far from each other. A wise man will fully understand all I have said. A fool will chase the wind and die in its grasp. Are you the wise man who gains knowledge, or the fool who dies? I will say no more."

While there were more questions that needed to be asked, it was obvious they would not be answered today or likely any other day. Sue was finished. Williams stood, took a final look at the woman, and walked out the door. He had more information than what he'd come with, but would it unveil him as a fool or lift him to the status of a wise man?

ACE COLLINS

CHAPTER 20

Saturday, April 24, 1942
2:15 PM
Outside Drury, Maryland

Alison Meeker, her hair blowing in the spring wind, parked the 1936 Packard Sedan outside the home that served as the headquarters for her sister's team. Grabbing a notebook, the teen quickly exited the car and hurried to the front entry. She'd no more than knocked when her sister pulled the door open.

"It's great to see you," Meeker announced, giving her a long hug. "That's a beautiful yellow suit. I think there used to be one just like it hanging in my closest."

"It's my apartment now," Alison jabbed with a grin, "and my closet. What you didn't take with you, I've claimed as my own. But let's put the talk of wardrobe off to another time. I have information I need to share. Since I don't trust the phones, I drove out to give it to you."

"Follow me to the living room," Meeker suggested. "We

can sit on the couch, and you can give me whatever is important enough to drag you away from Washington."

"Lead the way."

Once they were seated, Alison looked deeply into her sister's dark blue eyes and smiled. "Wish we had more time together. This war's kind of messing things up."

"Yeah. Becca and I were talking about how much our priorities have changed. I wonder if things will ever be back the way they used to be."

"Some things don't change," Alison assured her. "Yesterday, a young hotshot pilot asked me if I was rationed."

"Rationed? What does that mean?"

"You're still lost in old lingo," the young woman laughed. "You've got to get in step, Helen. If a girl is rationed, it means she's going steady."

"Oh, good to know. Was this pilot good-looking?"

"He was a dreamboat, a real killer-diller."

"And that's good?"

"Of course. But I came here to tell you news from the skyscraper."

"What a minute, Alison. I'm not sure what that means either."

"News from the top…you know, FDR."

"Ah, well, sister, give me the word before I run out of gas."

"Hey, you're stealing my thunder!"

Meeker grinned. "Just trying to stay up. Now, what did the president want me to know?"

"There's an agent at the FBI named James Killpatrick."

"I know him; he's one of Hoover's right-hand men. He has

a knack for coming up with information that's completely off the grid. He's the Hedda Hopper of the FBI."

"Well," Alison continued, "Killpatrick put a bug in Hoover's ear that Clay Barnes was spotted in Brownsville after he was supposedly killed in the plane crash. Naturally Hoover brought that information straight up the elevator to the White House. You follow that?"

"I got it," Meeker said as she slumped against the couch. "But who could have known Clay was in Brownsville. He was low-profile the whole time. In fact, he was seen by no one at all that could have tied him to the Secret Service."

"Are you sure?"

"Wait, sis," Meeker whispered. "Fister probably saw him. But how did the FBI get information on something Alistar Fister saw?"

"How did the FBI find out your grave was empty? That was the other bombshell Hoover dropped on the president."

Meeker felt her eyes go wide. "How did he answer?"

"He explained there was simply not enough of you left to bury. You had all but completely burned in the crash."

"What did the president tell Hoover about Clay?"

"He told him that Secret Service agents were chosen based on the fact they looked like average Americans and would always blend in. Therefore there were hundreds of men in the country who looked like Barnes."

"Those answers buy us some time," Meeker said with relief, "but they don't come close to explaining where Killpatrick's information came from."

"I've been letting that percolate on my drive out. I've got a crazy theory."

"Give it to me."

"What if the double agent and the mole is Killpatrick? The president told me the same thing you did, that the guy is always getting information no one else knows. What if his playing hero is really all about covering the fact he's actually a double agent?"

"Okay, that is wild," Meeker admitted, "but not so crazy it couldn't be true. Now let me toss one back at you." She got up and walked over to the window. As she spelled out her theory, her eyes fell on the yellow Packard she so loved. "Alistar saw Barnes in Texas, but so did Grace Lupino. What if Lupino is the double agent? What if she set Fister up? What if she took the documents to get them back to the United States government? What if she recognized me when I was in her dressing room? What if her contact is Killpatrick? And what if the man who's using Alistar only thinks Lupino is on his side?"

"Helen, that's a lot of what-ifs."

"So," Meeker said as she turned to face her sister, "I'll add one more. What if we're both right and Lupino is the good guy and Killpatrick is the bad guy?"

Alison shook her head. "We're going to need a meteorologist to figure out which direction the wind's blowing in this case."

CHAPTER 21

Saturday, April 24, 1942
10:15 PM
Washington D.C.

Alistar Fister got off the eastbound train at a quarter after ten. Stopping by a restroom, he checked his red beard and wig before wandering over to the information desk. As per instructions, he asked if there was a package or letter for David Waldorp. The attractive brunette behind the desk nodded, reached into a file drawer, and retrieved a business-sized envelope. After thanking her, Fister strolled over to a bench. After making sure no one was watching, he opened the letter. Though it was written in code, he easily deciphered his instructions.

Easing into his role as Riley O'Mally, he hailed a cab and caught a ride to Alexander Street. He had the driver stop two blocks before his final destination, and after paying the man, tipping him enough to look generous but not so much as to make a lasting impression, Fister got out, retrieved his bag, and ambled slowly toward Grace Lupino's apartment complex. Taking a position in an alley directly across the street from the building's main entrance, he pulled a thirty-eight revolver from his jacket pocket and waited for the singer to return home.

As it was well after most in the neighborhood had gone to bed and the area's two businesses were closed, the streets were deserted. Leaning against a brick wall bathed in a mixture of shadows and the glow of a streetlamp, Fister studied a white cat chasing bugs on the other side of Alexander Street. The animal seemed to have little interest in actually eating what he killed; for him it was all about the hunt. As he observed the energized feline, Fister smiled. He and the cat were cut from the same mold.

The man's attention was diverted from the cat-and-bug game when a 1940 Ford Deluxe sedan rolled down the street and stopped a half-block north of Lupino's building. With little but a passing interest, Fister observed a stylishly dressed woman step from the car. She looked to be around five-four, with a trim, almost athletic figure, and dark hair. Her suit fit like a glove, and she carried a handbag large enough to use as a travel case. As she walked in front of the closed drugstore's neon sign, his heart stopped.

"Helen," he whispered. How could she be walking the streets? She was dead! He'd read the articles on the plane crash and even celebrated her passing with a fifth of scotch.

Suddenly there was nothing else in the world but him and the woman who turned down his advances and ruined his plans. She'd brought him humiliation and shame and was the reason he had to reprove himself to Bauer. She'd almost cost him his life.

Fister's cool, calm demeanor instantly shifted into a hot, uncalculated rage. His lust for blood and need for revenge overruled his training and intelligence. He was no longer a human; he had become an animal living solely for revenge. With the smell of blood in the air, he was ready to move in for the kill.

After checking the silencer, he raised his gun, toyed with the trigger, and silently counted the woman's steps as she neared the apartment building. He determined he'd have a clear shot when she was a dozen feet from the building and just beyond a metal mailbox. That was the moment when she would again be in the light, and with her face illuminated, he would put a bullet through her brain.

"Five," he whispered as he steadied his arm by leaning against the corner of a brick wall, "four, three, two..."

Fister was concentrating so hard on his personal need for retribution he'd failed to notice the tall figure that had silently stolen up behind him. Just as he was about to squeeze the trigger, a large, strong arm grabbed the gun and jerked it out of his hand. The startled shooter quickly turned to fight off his attacker when a voice he knew well whispered, "We have plans for her."

"Bauer. What are you doing here?"

Only after Meeker made her way through the building's entrance did Bauer hand the gun back to Fister. He then stepped back into the alley and signaled for his gunman to follow. When they were a dozen feet from the street, he finally explained.

"I was in the area and wanted to watch this go down. It was fortunate I got here in time to stop you from making a mistake that would have cost you your life."

"That was Helen Meeker," Fister argued. "She deserves to die for the things she's done to me."

"Alistar," Bauer hissed, "this is not about personal revenge. We only kill people because it makes our job easier. Obviously Meeker is alive. There has to be a reason they faked her death. So what is it? We need to know that before we kill her. When we really need her dead, I'll give you first crack at it, but right now we need to concentrate on this mission. And with Meeker in the building and likely waiting to visit with our target, we'll have to wait a bit."

"But why would she be waiting for Grace?"

"Likely for the same reason we are. Let's see how this plays out. We have to find out where the package you lost is located before we take out Lupino. So when Meeker leaves—and only when she leaves—we'll move on it."

Bauer took a deep breath and placed his hand on Fister's shoulder. "Now, are you calmed down enough to do this job, or do I have to send you on your way and do it myself?"

"I can do it."

"I think it might be best if we do this one together," Bauer suggested. "Let's walk back up to the entrance of the alley and wait for Miss Lupino to come home. Then we can adjust our plans as needed."

Not more than five minutes after the pair took positions in the shadows by the sidewalk, a cab pulled up in front of the Red Rose Apartments. A stylishly dressed woman wearing a large hat slipped out of the back seat, nervously looked around, and gave

THE DEVIL'S EYES *In the President's Service Series: Episode 5*

the driver his fare. A few seconds later, she opened the front door and disappeared into the building.

"Now we wait," Bauer noted. "When Meeker comes out, we move in. In the meantime, I'm going to take a walk up the sidewalk and see if anyone else is watching this scene play out. You stay here."

Fister observed his boss slide his hands into the trench coat and amble toward the drugstore. By all appearances, the tall man looked like a local on a constitutional walk. For an instant, Fister considered pulling out his gun and killing the man who so controlled his life. But without Bauer, there was no future, at least not for Alistar Fister. And more than anything else, Fister wanted time to even the score with Helen Meeker.

CHAPTER 22
Saturday, April 24, 1942
11:45 PM

Bobbs had done her part in this mission just after the songbird left the apartment for the club. Thanks to the blonde's work, the place was set to fill with smoke as soon as Helen Meeker clicked on the table lamp beside the loveseat. But who knew when that would be? So for the moment, there was nothing to do but wait in the dark and listen to the rhythmic ticking of a mantel clock. Five minutes became ten and ten twenty, and to the guest the clock got louder and louder with each passing moment. As Meeker wasn't good at sitting still, she was ready to climb the walls when she finally heard the clicking of high heels in the hallway. A few seconds later, a key entered the latch and the door swung open. After tossing her purse onto a chair, Lupino flipped on the overhead light. An instant later, she recognized she wasn't alone.

"You!" she snarled.

"Close the door," Meeker suggested. "Then come over here and take a seat opposite me in that pink chair. I want to make sure you're comfortable while we talk."

"Why should I?" Lupino demanded.

"Because you know I carry a gun, and you have to believe I know how to use it."

The singer momentarily considered the warning before shutting the entry and sashaying over to the chair. She slithered into her seat, crossed her legs, folded her hands in her lap, and waited on the woman who was calling the shots. She didn't have to wait long.

"Gal, let's cut through all the bunk and get right to the point. There are at least two different organizations watching your every move. One of them is a mobster. Do you have any idea who he is?"

"I have nothing to do with organized crime," Lupino calmly replied. "If some hood is watching me, it's only because of the way I move my hips. Men like that. You should try it, and maybe you wouldn't be spending your Saturday nights alone."

Meeker smirked. The woman had moxie, and it was time to knock some of that out of her.

"I doubt if Lucky's eyes are good enough to see you from his prison cell." She allowed the image to fully develop before continuing. "And then there are those eyes that have connections to the Nazis. I suppose you'll tell me they're watching you because Hitler also loves to see you walk down the street."

Lupino's face contorted. "Who are you?"

"The person who's trying to save your pale hide. But to do it

I'm going to need some help."

"I don't need your help," the singer shot back.

"Oh, you think the package is your bulletproof shield, do you? What happens when someone finds where you've hidden it? Then what's your life worth? I can tell you what it's worth sister. Nothing!"

"I've still got it," Lupino spat back.

"I have no doubt of that. But you're playing this gig solo against two of the most ruthless and powerful forces in the world. I don't know how you're going to sleep at night with all those eyes on you."

"And which of them are you working for?"

"Uncle Sam. He's the player that makes this spy song a trio for you."

"My uncle can't protect me, but what my uncle wants guarantees I keep breathing. You see, it works no matter who's warbling the tune or taking the lead part."

There was no use pursuing this anymore. It was obvious the dialogue was meaningless. It was time to rely on a bit of Hollywood magic.

"Let's shed a bit more light on this," Meeker suggested as she reached over and pushed the lamp switch. She silently counted to ten before asking, "Do you smell smoke?"

Bobbs had set things up for the fire to appear to begin in the kitchen, so Meeker turned her gaze that way. As she did, Lupino's eyes followed. As she noted the smoke, her eyes grew large and wild. She was taking the bait.

"We better get out of here," Meeker suggested. "It's coming

out of your bedroom too. All the stuff you have crowded in here makes it a tinderbox. This place'll be consumed in minutes."

As the smoke crept into the living room, Lupino's face showed real panic. Leaping to her feet, she pushed her hands into her dark hair and attempted to scream, but not a sound came through her lips. Playing it to the hilt, Meeker jumped off the loveseat and hurried to the front door. After opening it, she looked back into the smoke that was now rolling across the floor.

"Come on, sister, let's take flight."

Lupino's head seemed to be on a swivel as she took inventory of all she was about to lose. As the seconds ticked by and the smoke rose higher, it was obvious she was torn between rushing out with Meeker and staying to fight the blaze.

"Come on, Gal," Meeker urged.

"Just a second," the singer shouted back.

"That's about all you have," Meeker yelled.

As Lupino rushed into her bedroom, Meeker stepped back into the living room to observe what had given the singer enough courage to face what she assumed was raging fire. Racing to the corner, her heels clicking on the hardwood floor, the panicked songbird grabbed a floor lamp. The light standard had a thick barrel base. After yanking off the shade, Lupino began to untwist the top. When she had the top loose, she picked up the heavy, five-foot high base and turned it over. As she did, a cardboard tube fell onto the smoke-covered floor.

Smiling, Meeker turned and moved back to the entry and waited for the singer. A few seconds later, the raven-haired beauty sprinted out of the bedroom, across the living room, and out the door.

"Come on, dear," Meeker suggested, "let's get out of this place. I've got a car parked just down the street. There's a fire alarm beside it."

Meeker led the way down the steps and pushed open the front door. Stepping to one side, she made room for the frightened singer to rush by. As Lupino made her way into the cool night air, Meeker wrestled the tube away. With the documents in one hand and her Colt in the other, she smiled. "There's a dark blue 1940 Ford sedan up by the drugstore. That's where we're going."

A breathless Lupino looked from the gun to the tube, her face a kaleidoscope of expressions, then turned and began to walk to the Ford. She was halfway there when a wide-shouldered man surprised both the singer and Meeker by quickly stepping from a 1940 La Salle. He held a forty-five in his right hand.

"The dame's mine," he growled. "Come on, sweetheart, get in the car."

"I've got a bigger gun than yours," Meeker noted.

"The lady comes prepared," the man replied. "Looks like we have a stand-off."

"Brother, it would be best if you just put yourself and that ugly tweed jacket back in the car and roared off into the night. That way you get out of here without my ventilating the coat and your chest."

"And why is that, lady? What gives you the right to talk so tough?"

"Because I have back up." She smiled. "And I know Rocko Wells always works alone."

The light from the drugstore's neon sign caught the man's lopsided grin. "You not only bring firepower, but you do your homework. You must have been a Girl Scout. You win, sister. I'm getting back in my car."

"Not until you drop the gun on the street."

"You're calling the shots," Wells said with a shrug. After carefully placing the forty-five on the sidewalk, he backed through the passenger side door of his bloated, heavily chromed sedan. A second later, three shots rang out.

Meeker dove down behind Wells' car for cover and peered between the La Salle and an older model Hudson to gauge where the shooter or shooters were hiding. Using the confusion, the private investigator pulled Lupino by the collar into his car. Within seconds he'd started the La Salle, yanked into first, spun the wheel to the left, and driven onto Alexander Street, scraping the Hudson's back fender. Once in the street, he made a U-turn and sped north.

Her Colt in one hand, the cardboard tube in the other, Meeker rolled toward the drugstore until she had cover from a Dodge truck. A few seconds later, the 1938 Ford delivery truck pulled up to the curb and the passenger door flew open. Not waiting for an invitation, Meeker dove into the seat beside Becca Bobbs. Even before the door closed, Clay Barnes hit the gas, spun the wheel, and put the truck into a one-eighty spin to join in hot pursuit of Wells.

"You okay?" Bobbs asked.

"I'm fine, and I've got the tube. Who fired those shots?"

"The shots came from that alley to the right, where we're

THE DEVIL'S EYES *In the President's Service Series: Episode 5*

about to pass," the blonde explained.

As Meeker glanced through the truck's glass, it was as if time had slowed to a crawl. Her senses, heightened by the gunshots, were so keen that even in the darkness her blue eyes could see everything around her in precise detail. As one of the likely shooters stepped closer to the Ford, her gaze intensified. At this moment there were no other people on the planet, as even those in the truck with her evaporated into an invisible mist.

The man stood with his arms at his side and his feet about shoulder-width apart. He was tall and dressed in a dark coat and slacks. As if frozen by the glow of a street lamp, his dark, foreboding eyes locked so intensely on Meeker it sent a chill racing down her spine and digging so deeply into her heart she couldn't catch her breath. It was as if somehow his fist were squeezing the very life from her body.

"You recognize either of the shooters?" Barnes asked, jumpstarting time and yanking Meeker back from her seeming supernatural trance.

As the man disappeared behind them, Meeker rubbed her neck as if that simple act would help stop the still lingering cold chill encasing her body. "I think I just saw the face of the devil," she said, "and somehow he knows me."

To be continued...............

ACE COLLINS

Made in the USA
Middletown, DE
09 May 2017